W9-DII-945

THE Way We Were

Center Point
Large Print

**This Large Print Book carries the
Seal of Approval of N.A.V.H.**

THE Way We Were

Judy Baer

CENTER POINT PUBLISHING
THORNDIKE, MAINE

This Center Point Large Print edition
is published in the year 2009 by arrangement with
GuidepostsBooks.

The text of this Large Print edition is unabridged.
In other aspects, this book may vary
from the original edition.
Printed in the United States of America.
Set in 16-point Times New Roman type.

ISBN: 978-1-60285-357-7

Library of Congress Cataloging-in-Publication Data

Baer, Judy.
  The way we were / Judy Baer.
    p. cm.
  ISBN 978-1-60285-357-7 (lib. bdg. : alk. paper)
  1. Bed and breakfast accommodations--Fiction. 2. Pennsylvania--Fiction.
   3. Amnesia--Fiction. 4. Marital conflict--Fiction. 5. Large type books. I. Title.

PS3552.A33W39 2009
813'.54--dc22

2008040105

Acknowledgments

In memory of Ann Fox. And for Casey, Sarah, Erin, Amber and Ashley Fox. She will be remembered.

—Judy Baer

Chapter One

"Where do you think she is?" asked Louise Howard Smith from her seat on the porch of Grace Chapel Inn. She peered down Chapel Road, and then leaned back in her white wicker rocker. Picking up a frosted glass, she took a sip of icy lemonade. "It's not like Alice to be late."

"Something must have held her up at the hospital," her sister Jane said. Jane crossed her khaki-clad legs and wiggled her toes, revealed by a pair of rubber flip-flops, admiring her freshly painted toenails. "Frankly, I'm enjoying the chance to put my feet up. I don't mind having dinner a bit late."

Louise nodded, her perfectly coiffed silver hair gleaming in the sun. Her blue eyes matched the sky blue of her blouse, which had a lace hankie peeking daintily from its pocket.

They gazed languidly at the quiet street, relishing their idleness. A peaceful hour on the porch during a summer afternoon was a luxury ever since they'd made their childhood home in Acorn Hill, Pennsylvania, into a popular bed-and-breakfast. Usually they would be engaged in the care of the inn's guests.

"It's been busy at the inn, hasn't it?" Louise said, sighing. Grace Chapel Inn had been full nearly every day for the past several weeks. "I'm not complaining, mind you, but I am a little tired. Sometimes I don't know how Alice does it, working at the hospital in Potterston and helping out here as well."

"She loves it." Jane gave her older sister a heavy-lidded glance. "You know she does. And I do too. Coming home to Acorn Hill to be with you and Alice at the inn is one of the best decisions I've ever made. I can hardly wait to introduce my friends to this wonderful place."

Louise was about to respond when Alice's car turned the corner and came up the driveway at an unusually fast clip.

"Who lit a fire under her?" Jane murmured.

Alice turned her small blue Toyota into the inn's parking lot and stepped out, pushing the door closed behind her. Her red-brown hair shone in the sunlight, and her brown eyes were aglow with excitement. Louise and Jane glanced at each other, then back at Alice.

Alice hurried to the porch and up the steps.

"Hi, dear. Pull up a chair and relax," Jane said. She leaned forward and patted the padded rocker next to hers. "You look as though you've heard exciting news. Tell us what it is."

"Exciting? Well, I'm not sure I'd say that . . . except in a medical sense, I suppose. In all my years of nursing, I've seen so little of this that it is, well . . ." Alice flushed and put her hands to her cheeks, "stimulating."

8

"Maybe I should get you a glass of lemonade," Jane suggested.

"That would be wonderful." Alice fluttered a hand in front of her face. "It really is warm this afternoon."

Jane glanced at Louise, who was smiling. Alice was normally a very composed woman. It wasn't often that she was so keyed up. Jane disappeared into the house and returned with a glass and a pitcher, which she set on a low table in front of her sister.

Alice sipped her lemonade. "I don't believe I've ever worked with a patient with this diagnosis before."

"What is it?" Louise asked. "Are you allowed to tell us?"

"Oh yes. This patient wants *everyone* to know what her difficulty is. She is encouraging us to share her story."

"Just what is this remarkable condition?" Jane asked, urging her sister along.

"Amnesia."

"You have a patient with amnesia?" Jane sat forward in her chair.

"I didn't know that actually happened," Louise said.

"It's quite rare, I imagine," Jane said.

"That's what makes it so interesting." Alice nodded. "This is a textbook case." She took a sip of lemonade and continued. "There are two basic kinds of amnesia—anterograde and retrograde. Anterograde amnesia is the inability to remember events *after* the trauma or disease that caused it. New events in the immediate memory aren't transferred to the permanent, long-term memory. It's why so many people, after an accident, say that they can't remember a thing about what happened to them when they were hurt.

"Retrograde amnesia causes people to be unable to recall events that occurred *before* the onset of the amnesia. Sometimes both can occur in the same patient."

"Trent Vescio, my old boss in San Francisco, had a motorcycle accident," Jane said. "He woke up at the hospital unable to remember that he'd even been driving his bike. I went to see him, as did several other people from the Blue Fish Grille, but when he came back to work, he admitted that he couldn't remember any of us being there."

"He recovered, didn't he?" Louise asked.

"Oh yes," Jane said, smiling. "He still doesn't remember anything surrounding the accident, but everything else is there."

Alice frowned. "What's troubling about this woman is that she is exhibiting total memory loss about her past and everything leading up to and just after the accident. It's as if she never had a childhood, a family or a history of any kind. She doesn't know if she's married or has children. She doesn't even know her own name."

"Oh dear." Louise put on the wire-rimmed glasses that hung from a chain around her neck. Though her sisters teased her about it, Louise felt that she could hear better when she wore her glasses. "That poor woman."

"I'm concerned that if the amnesia continues much longer it might be a sign that it's going to be permanent." Alice took a sip of her lemonade. "I know Mary—that's what we're calling her—would appreciate your prayers."

"You know she'll have them," Louise said.

"Yes, of course," Jane added. "How frightening it must be to wake up and not know who you are."

"For some reason, it feels as if God has placed me in Mary's life. I want to do what I can."

"Do you know about what happened to her?" Jane asked.

"It's the strangest thing. She was found on the side of a rural road not far from Acorn Hill, just past Fairy Pond. There was no car around and no sign of how she got there. She had a very nasty bruise on her head, a black eye, and numerous contusions, cuts and abrasions. Her shoulder was dislocated and she had a lot of dirt and gravel embedded in her arm and leg. The doctor said she could have been in a car accident, or maybe she had been hiking and had taken a serious fall. Of course we have no real idea what happened."

Louise practically clucked with dismay.

"If it hadn't been for the dog, no one knows how

long she might have lain by the side of the road."

Both Louise and Jane looked at her in surprise. "What dog?" they asked nearly in unison.

"Finnias, an Irish setter. He's called Finn for short. Apparently Finn discovered Mary and sat down by her side. I think you know his owner, Kieran Morgan. When Kieran noticed that Finn hadn't come home, he went out looking for him. Kieran called Finn when he saw him up ahead on the road, but Finn refused to come. So Mr. Morgan went to the dog to lead him to his truck and found Mary lying unconscious in the grass," Alice said. "The dog is a real hero."

"Amazing," Jane said in a whisper, caught up in Alice's story. "To be saved by a dog. It's hard to imagine."

"What will happen to her?" Louise wondered aloud. "What if she *doesn't* remember who she is?"

"Right now she has to stay in the hospital. The doctor is worried about a concussion. But when she's ready to leave, I'm not sure where she'll go, especially if she has no idea where she belongs."

"No wonder you were so agitated when you arrived, Alice. You've had quite an extraordinary day."

"I've been praying that Mary's memory returns quickly." Alice always prayed for her patients, believing that the Great Physician was the One who could heal the soul and the body. "And I've been trying to think of ways to get her story out."

"Why does she want everyone to know her problem?" Louise asked.

"She's hoping someone will come forward and tell her who she is," Alice said, her voice sad.

"Of course," Louise said. "Well, it's too late for this week's *Acorn Nutshell*. I'm sure Carlene has the edition all laid out. But perhaps you can check with Mary and see if she'd like the idea of an article in the newspaper next week."

"Yes, I'll do that."

"Why don't you put Ethel and Florence on the case? Those two are better than television for spreading the news." Jane smiled. "That's how Lloyd does it when he wants lots of people at a city council meeting. He tells Ethel, who tells Florence, who tells everyone she knows, who tell everyone they know."

Louise laughed. "And the town hall is bursting at the seams by seven in the evening."

Ethel Buckley was their much-loved aunt, the half-sister of Daniel Howard, the sisters' late father. Widowed, Ethel lived next door in the inn's carriage house and popped in to visit almost as regularly as a clock reads noon and midnight. She and her friend Florence Simpson, a well-to-do woman in the community, were, for the most part, benevolent gossips. Getting to know everything about everyone had become a hobby for them, like stamp collecting. Of course neither Ethel nor Florence was wired for a sedate leisure pursuit like philately.

"Perhaps you should go upstairs and take a shower to relax you before dinner, Alice," Jane suggested gently. "You've had a difficult day. We're having a cold supper: ham, rolls, broccoli-and-cauliflower salad, and fresh tomatoes with mozzarella and basil. I'll put it out, and we'll eat when you're ready."

Tenderly, Alice put her hand on Jane's cheek. "You are such a blessing. Thanks for taking such good care of me."

Jane rose from her chair to gather her sister in her arms. "You have so much compassion for people that sometimes I'm afraid you'll simply wear out from giving of yourself."

"I'm just passing it along," Alice said with a smile. "God gives generously to me, and I hand it on to someone else."

"And it appears that Mary may be the next lucky recipient of your gifts."

Alice laughed. "God did practically toss her into my lap."

After Alice had gone upstairs, Louise helped Jane set the table in the kitchen.

"It sounds as though Alice has a new project on her hands," Louise said as she laid out napkins.

"No doubt this woman will need someone on her side," Jane said as she sliced a tomato. "I can't think of anyone better than our sister."

Chapter Two

Louise had gone upstairs to freshen up before dinner, and as Jane waited for her sisters to join her, she sampled the salad she'd made, savoring the creamy taste of the dressing. There was just enough vinegar, the merest hint of dry mustard—perfect. One of the things she was most grateful for about running the inn was that she could use her culinary abilities to please others. A professional chef, she'd turned her formidable talent toward the kitchen at Grace Chapel Inn, making their bed-and-breakfast a favored destination for travelers in that part of Pennsylvania. She'd become an expert at creating delicious breakfasts, and guests rarely missed that meal. In addition to traditional fare, Jane offered things such as pannekuken, chili con huevos, crème brûlée, Scandinavian fruit soup, brioches and chocolate pecan strudel.

Jane looked around her professional-grade kitchen. Being a chef in a country inn wasn't the life she'd envisioned for herself early in her career. She wasn't presiding over the kitchen in her own trendy restaurant or living in a sleek, contemporary apartment with a view of San Francisco. And she wasn't wearing designer clothing and jewelry— unless you considered that she had designed much of her clothing and costume jewelry herself. Nor was she supporting herself with her art. How did she measure up to the vision she'd had for herself when she left art school to tackle the world?

She was happy, contented and sure that God had put her in this place for a reason. That is what counted most, even if she didn't appear outwardly successful, not, at least, by the standards of her former college roommates.

A flutter of anticipation went through her. Her old college friends were due at the inn the next afternoon for a five-night stay. It would be the first reunion the four of them had had together in far too many years.

Jane recalled the little yellow house they'd rented during their second year of art school. It was an old, tiny place in a semirun-down part of town that was slowly being gentrified. The girls had loved the ethnic atmosphere of the area with wonderful little mom-and-pop shops and great family restaurants. They'd all been so proud to be completely independent and on their own.

"You're daydreaming again," Louise said as she and Alice entered the kitchen. "You've been particularly pensive lately. Are you excited about this reunion of yours?"

Louise was right, Jane decided as she waved to her sisters to take a seat at the table. Jane had been giving the visit a great deal of thought. It was normal, Jane suspected, to be a bit uneasy when it had been so many years—and miles—since she and her friends had been together. Would they be strangers or would they fall easily into old patterns of friendship?

"Refresh my memory. It's been a long time since we've talked about your friends. Tell us again about them when you were all in school," Alice said as she sat down in one of the wooden chairs. "You were always so busy back then that we had a difficult time keeping up with you."

"First, let's say grace," Louise suggested, placing her napkin in her lap.

The sisters bowed their heads, and Louise began. "Dear Heavenly Father, thank You for this food and for the person who cooked it. Jane is so special to us, so generous, loving and creative. We ask that You particularly bless her this week and that the reunion will be an opportunity to glorify You. And we pray for Mary, that she find not only her health but her identity. Keep her from being afraid. In Your name we pray."

"Amen," the three sisters chorused.

Alice enthusiastically spooned a helping of salad onto her plate.

Louise split open a fragrant dinner roll and looked expectantly at Jane. "Now let's hear those stories."

"Stella, Patty, Becky and I are four distinct personalities. Sometimes I'm surprised we got along at all. Other times I realize that our differences are what made us so close." Jane took a sip of water before continuing.

"Patty and Becky tended to be more reserved—in crowds, at least—while Stella and I were always up for a party."

"Some things just never change," Louise murmured.

"Hey!" Jane nudged her sister's arm. "You aren't averse to parties yourself."

Jane glanced out the window toward the carriage house as if seeing something from the past. "Soon after we all moved into the little house we rented off campus, Stella and I gave a party, and, oh what a party it was! Patty and Becky told us we could never have another—at least of that magnitude."

"Do tell," Louise encouraged.

"We decided to have a housewarming. We'd known each other the year before, but hung out in different crowds. Becky and I had a lot of mutual friends, and Stella and Patty knew each other from several classes they'd shared. Becky and I had discussed rooming together, as had Stella and Patty. Two of us couldn't afford anything very nice, but together we were able to rent the house. We thought a party would give all our friends a chance to meet one another. Besides, considering the tiny dorm rooms we'd been living in the year before, our place seemed like a mansion, and we were eager to show it off."

Jane cleared her throat. "Turns out it was not quite big enough for the party we gave. Becky and Patty thought we should each plan a guest list so we knew how many would be coming, but Stella and I figured that no matter how many people we invited, a number of them wouldn't be able to come. We decided it would be safer, like the airlines, to 'overbook' the guests rather than have an empty house."

"Oh dear," Alice murmured. "I'm glad you got over that idea before you came back to help run the inn."

"I learned my lesson, believe me. The grocery store was advertising ridiculously cheap frozen pizzas as a loss leader, so I bought twenty of them, figuring that what we didn't eat at the party, we would finish later."

"Twenty pizzas?" Louise said in mock sternness. "No wonder you were always so pleased when one of us sent you a bit of extra money. Even then you were spending it on food."

Jane laughed. "Yes, I guess so. Well, anyway, we went out and invited everyone we knew. Becky, Patty and I didn't know it, but Stella also told everyone she invited to bring a friend. That night our little house was full by the time the party was to start and people were in the basement, on the porch and spilling into the yard. My twenty pizzas were gone in half an hour and I had to run to the store for twenty more."

"How many people came to this party? Forty pizzas?" Alice marveled.

"We lost count at one hundred and fifty."

Jane's sisters both set down their forks on the table and stared at her.

She shrugged cheerfully. "Stella took a collection for the next round of pizzas. Everyone was happy to contribute because we were having such a good time. Stella collected so much that I had enough left over to buy ice cream and chocolate syrup. Anyone with a sweet tooth had to take a turn having dessert, of course, because we had only a limited number of bowls and glasses. Patty stood at the sink washing used glassware and dishes while Becky dried them and Stella and I filled them up again. We felt like the lunch ladies at school by the time the evening was over."

"But what happened? With all those people, I mean?"

"They all had a great time, played volleyball in the backyard, got to know each other and eventually—in the middle of the night—went home. The next week one of the guests sent us a coupon for a free pizza and said it was the best party she'd ever attended."

"So you pulled it off?"

"We did. Stella and I got into some trouble with our roommates, however. They said no more parties of more than fifty people, and I got strict instructions that if I was ever going to serve ice cream again, I'd have to provide disposable bowls."

"We knew you loved people, Jane, but a hundred and fifty . . ." Louise shook her head.

"It was a great way to start the year," Jane said. "I knew a lot more people on campus after that."

Louise stood up to refill their water glasses, and when she sat down, she said, "I'm surprised you didn't get into trouble with your landlord over that one."

"Actually, we'd invited his daughter to the party, and she had a wonderful time."

Jane leaned back in her chair and an impish smile graced her features. "We did have a problem with our landlord concerning something else, though."

Her sisters leaned forward, waiting for what she would say next.

"It served the landlord right, actually. He had no business sneaking around the house after dark."

"What?" Louise and Alice said in unison.

Jane put down her fork. "Not 'sneaking,' exactly, but how were the rest of us to know that Patty had called him to report a leak in the outside faucet? Becky, who was in the bedroom studying, heard something scratching outside her window. She was very excitable in those days anyway, and there had been a cat burglar reported only a couple of miles away, so she decided the noise was the burglar. She got on her hands and knees and crawled out the bedroom door, found Stella and me in the living room and told us we had to do something."

"Did you call the police?" Alice asked.

"I did, but Stella has a real creative streak. While I was on the telephone, she talked Becky into helping her. They took a big blanket and tiptoed outside. They saw a man kneeling on the ground, head down, looking into our basement window. They got close enough to throw the blanket over him and they were still struggling with him when the police arrived."

Alice put her hand to her heart.

"*That's* when we got in trouble with our landlord. He was just trying to fix the faucet and, since Patty had called him, he didn't think it necessary to warn us that he was coming."

Jane's eyes twinkled at the memory. "When they threw the blanket over him, he bumped his eye on the faucet handle, and it had started turning black and blue. It took the police quite a while to straighten out the mess. It wasn't until Patty came home and told them she was the one who'd called our landlord and identified him that they decided not to arrest him."

"I would have had a heart attack if I'd known all this was going on!" Louise exclaimed.

"It was just good college fun," Jane said. "He threatened to raise our rent but finally had to admit he should have alerted us before he came over."

"Well, as disturbing as that little story was, I'm beginning to get a picture of your friends," Louise commented.

Jane imagined Stella as she'd last seen her. It had been at Stella's wedding, a lavish affair. She'd married a man much older than herself, Al Leftner, an art gallery owner who, over the years, had featured and sold much of Stella's work. She'd known Al as a business collaborator for many years, but it wasn't until she was in her late thirties that they had realized they'd fallen in love.

"Stella is a wealthy woman," Jane commented aloud. "Her artwork has received a lot of recognition, much of it thanks to her husband's gallery. He's a very prosperous man. They've never had children, so her husband and her work have always been her main concerns."

"Is he the one with the sailboat and the small island?" Louise asked. "The one in the photo you received in a Christmas card one year?"

"That's Al."

"Oh my, do you think the inn will be good enough for her?" Alice's forehead creased in a frown.

"I know it will be. Although Stella has money, she's not a snob. She's more impressed by warmth and coziness than she is with cold elegance." Jane took a bite of salad, then continued. "Stella studied abroad during high school and summered with her aunt and uncle in their beach home in West Hampton, New York. Her relatives were 'very proper and very distant' she always said. The warmth and charm of the inn will be perfect. Stella will enjoy it here. Despite her upbringing—or Al's status—she's not likely to be critical or fussy." Jane laid down her fork. "About her surroundings, anyway."

"But she *is* critical and fussy about something, I take it?" Louise asked.

"Herself."

Louise's and Alice's eyebrows arched in surprise.

"When she was in college, Stella was very concerned about her weight and her looks, though she was slender and beautiful. I remember telling her once that I'd tallied up all she'd eaten one semester and it amounted to three bunches of celery, two bags of radishes and a crate of lettuce. She'd watch the rest of us eat fried chicken or mounds of take-out Chinese food and then tell us how fat she felt. We'd eat with gusto, going through a huge order of shrimp fried rice while she'd nibble on bok choy and bean sprouts. The rest of us would have loved to have looked as beautiful and put together as she, but none of us cared to put in as much effort as she did."

"That's probably for the best," Alice said.

"Becky was always *planning* to go on a diet, but she never actually got around to it. She was always bemoaning her round face and chubby cheeks, but she'd still have had those no matter how little she ate."

"Did Becky come from a wealthy family too?"

"No. Becky's father left the family when she was young, and she had to take on a lot of responsibility for her younger siblings at an early age."

Jane chuckled. "Becky was in an earth-mother stage in college and claimed that anything uncomfortable was unnatural. She threw out all her shoes except for a pair of clogs and some tennis shoes. As for clothing, if it wasn't pajamas, jeans or some dreadful granny dress, she wouldn't wear it."

"What about Patty?" Louise had forgotten about eating now, and was completely immersed in Jane's stories.

"She is an interior decorator and runs her own company. Her parents were in their forties when she was born. She also married a man several years older than herself. She has one stepchild, a boy."

"Such different personalities and lives," Louise murmured. "This will be a very interesting visit."

"I wonder if Stella still needs to be in control of everything," Jane mused.

"I imagine it was rather difficult to control you," Alice, the voice of experience, said. "I recall your having a very strong mind of your own."

A faint smile lit Jane's features. "Poor Stella. It was difficult to manage us. I remember the time she decided that we were all going to follow her beauty regimen for a month. We nearly drove her crazy. Becky would get up, throw on a long raincoat over her pajamas and go to class. I'd use all of Stella's products in the wrong order, and she'd lecture me about clogging my pores. Patty tried to follow Stella's instructions but never quite succeeded. Pretty soon Stella gave up on us and found projects that were more manageable."

"Stella sounds like an interesting character," Alice said.

"Stella was . . . is . . . complicated. Despite her talent and beauty, she was never very self-confident. Because she was always unsure of how things might turn out or what might happen, she wanted to be in control of every situation—and that included us."

"I wonder what she's like now," Louise buttered another roll as she spoke.

"So do I," Jane murmured.

"It sounds as though you all got along despite your differences," Louise said.

"For the most part. It wasn't always smooth sailing though."

"Why do you say that?" Alice asked.

"There was nothing big, but sometimes we got under each other's skin. Becky was a night owl who liked to sleep in. Patty was an up-with-the-birds sort of person. More than once, Becky sneaked into Patty's room after she'd gone to bed and turned off her alarm clock so that Patty wouldn't be up rustling around at five in the morning and wake her up."

"I suppose that didn't go over well," Louise said with a chuckle.

"The only thing that got everyone upset was the month or two that Stella decided that smoking was not only sophisticated, but also a great diet aid. She smelled up our house until a guy she was dating convinced her that the habit wasn't at all appealing. Thanks to him, she quit and never took it up again."

The kitchen door swung open and Aunt Ethel chugged purposefully into the room. Her face was flushed with excitement, and her Titian red hair looked as though she'd combed it in a hurry.

"Did you hear?" she blurted.

"Hear what?" Alice asked. Ethel had a tendency to be overly dramatic. She could just as easily be about to announce the news of an airplane landing on Hill Street as to report a new food item at the Good Apple Bakery.

"Alma Streeter, the Acorn Hill postmistress, has been called away to an emergency in her family."

"I hope nothing serious," Alice said.

"An ailing parent, I understand. Open-heart surgery, maybe, or a broken leg. I'm not sure which."

There was a difference between Ethel's diagnoses, but Jane and her sisters didn't point that out. Sometimes facts only got in the way of Ethel's fun.

Jane noticed her aunt eyeing the dinner table. "Would you like some dinner?"

Ethel pulled out a chair and sat down. "Just some of your wonderful salad, please. Oh, and a tiny bit of ham. Are those homemade rolls?"

Jane got up to get Ethel a plate and silverware, then rejoined her sisters at the table.

"Who'll be running the post office?" Louise asked as she handed the basket of rolls to her aunt.

"Someone from Pittsburgh or Philadelphia." Ethel cut her slice of ham. "She's starting tomorrow."

"That will be quite a change," Jane said, "from the big city to the little burg of Acorn Hill."

"She will, of course, need friends." Ethel practically beamed with purpose and goodwill.

"And that's where you come in?"

"Florence and I have already decided we should act as Acorn Hill's unofficial welcoming committee. Won't that be nice?"

"What inspired this idea?" Jane asked. *Why should Aunt Ethel be so interested in a substitute postal worker?* she wondered. Ethel had never been interested in the post office before except for what news and gossip she could learn in the lobby.

"A couple of things, really. Lloyd has been so busy with his mayoral duties that I thought I could help him out a bit by welcoming our new postmistress to the town."

That meant that because Lloyd was busy, Ethel had extra time on her hands. Ethel and Mayor Tynan ordinarily spent a lot of time together, and she often depended upon him to entertain her.

"My other inspiration is a Bible study Florence and I have been doing together."

"How nice." Alice said. "I didn't know you were doing that." Their aunt, despite her proclivity to gossip, was a sweet, sweet soul.

Ethel looked pleased with herself. "It's very good

for us. We're applying what we're studying, making it real, you might say."

"We were just talking about Jane's college room-mates who are coming tomorrow for a stay at the inn," Alice explained as they ate. "I'd like to hear more about the one who illustrates children's books. What fun that must be."

"Becky? You'll love her. She's such a sweet-heart and so good-natured. I can't remember her ever being anything but kind, compassionate and generous. She's always adored children and she is wonderful with them. She was the oldest of five, and she spent many hours reading stories to them. That experience might have influenced her decision to use her talent for children's illustra-tions."

"Does she have any children of her own?"

"Two girls and two boys. They're grown, of course, and out of the house." Jane laughed. "I remember when the last one went off to college. Becky said that, much as she loved him, it was rather nice not to compete with loud music in the house and to find food still in the refrigerator at the end of the day."

"I know exactly what she means," Ethel pro-nounced, "not on that scale, of course, but I have been inviting Lloyd for dinner since he's been so busy. I can't keep food in the house. He keeps telling me he has to eat to keep up his strength, that he's just a 'growing boy.'" She smiled fondly as if she could see him standing in front of her patting his ample tummy.

"Growing out, maybe, not up," Jane mumbled. Alice gave her a warning look.

All three sisters were glad that Lloyd Tynan was in their aunt's life. He kept her company, enriched her involvement in the community and made her laugh.

Ethel glanced at her watch. "I'd better go. I thought I might stop by the post office and say hello to the new postmistress. Thanks for the wonderful meal, Jane. I wish so often that you could have cooked for your mother. You remind me so much of her."

After she'd bustled out the door, Louise and Jane began to clear away the dishes.

"Aunt Ethel certainly has a lot of zeal for getting to know the new person in town," Louise murmured. "Did I detect even more enthusiasm than usual?"

"Although I'm not crazy about Ethel's love of gossip, I'd be more uncomfortable if she weren't curious," Jane observed. "It's in her blood. You know how much she loves to be invited to any function we're having here."

"She likes the food."

"Maybe, but she's even more eager to meet our guests, particularly those she thinks are 'important.'"

"Then, considering her interest, our newcomer

must be very important." Alice picked up a book that was lying on the kitchen counter and tucked it beneath her arm. "If you will excuse me, I think I'll go to bed now."

"So early?" Jane looked at her wristwatch. "It's only nine."

"Oh, I don't plan to go to sleep. I brought home some reading material on amnesia. I'm finding Mary's case quite fascinating."

"I'll be along shortly," Louise said. "I'm tired. I spent a lot of time practicing the organ today, and my back aches."

"Don't expect me to turn in early," Jane said. "I'd never be able to sleep anyway. I can't quit thinking about tomorrow."

Jane stayed up long after her sisters had gone to bed, looking at recipe books and listening to jazz.

Finally she laid one of Julia Child's tomes across her lap and stared out the window toward the garden in which she spent so much time. Her thoughts drifted again to her art school days and to the friends with whom she'd shared so much.

Slender and high-strung Stella with her model-perfect figure and long dark hair had been popular with men. But despite all the flattery, the flowers and the dates, Stella had been dreadfully hard on herself. Jane recalled her staring into the mirror on a hunt for imaginary imperfections. She'd change clothes a half-dozen times before a date and still leave frowning, sure she didn't look good enough. As Jane had told her sisters, Stella didn't like anything she couldn't control, and a flare-up of acne or an extra pound could upset her terribly. Jane suspected that Stella had battled with eating disorders back then.

"So lovely and so unhappy about it," Jane murmured to herself.

Patty had struggled, too, in her own way. She was obsessive about her class work. Stella did well in school without much effort. She was a true, natural talent and was always one of the professors' favorites. Patty, on the other hand, worked hard for every accomplishment. Tall, big-boned, slow-moving, meticulous, never-to-be-rushed Patty. Like Stella, she was also a beauty, but in a more natural, voluptuous way. She'd grown up in Texas and wore her blonde hair full and fluffy. Jeans and boots were her favorite default clothing.

Patty was doggedly persistent, and her projects were often notable in their creativity and beauty. Patty worked steadily until she achieved success while Stella sprinted ahead, claimed her accomplishments and went on to something else.

A memory flickered in Jane's mind, a shopping trip: Stella, in a bright blue wool pantsuit, her hair teased into a poufy bouffant and held back with a red, blue and yellow scarf, had herded them into a department store.

"We've got two hours to find each of you a new outfit. We'll have to hurry."

"I don't need anything new," Becky groused.

"I'm sorry, but something purchased at Goodwill is not appropriate for an art gallery. This is an opening! We have to be elegant, refined."

"Then you'll have to do more than buy me some new clothes," Patty said. "You're the elegant, refined one in this group. Besides, no matter what I wear I still have size eleven feet. The most beautiful shoes in the world look like canoes on me. I'd rather wear boots."

"Help me here, Jane, will you?" Stella had pleaded. "The four of us have been invited to a gallery opening by my art professor. There will be other artists there. And buyers! Not to mention a string quartet and canapés. I know you'll look perfect, but these two can't come looking like Ma Kettle and Calamity Jane."

It had been like pulling teeth but Stella had managed to convince them all that sequins were the *perfect* thing for an opening. As far as Jane could recall, they'd ended up at the gallery opening looking more like Diana Ross and the Supremes than aspiring art students.

Tall, curvy Patty was stunning, Jane remembered, but she told everyone she met that high heels were instruments of torture and Stella was abusing her by making her wear them.

Jane had enjoyed dressing up almost as much as

33

Stella. All in all, the night had been a success even though Becky and Patty refused, for many years, to admit it.

Grinning at the memory, Jane made herself a cup of tea and grabbed a handful of almonds. It was past her bedtime, but she found the quiet moments thinking about her friends to be soothing, a preparation for their arrival the following day.

Crunching on an almond, she returned to her post and continued to stare out the window.

It was Becky to whom Jane had been closest. She was so sweet-natured, compassionate and generous that Jane had been immediately attracted to her. Becky was born to mother and loved to take care of people, to comfort them and to tend to their needs. If anyone in the house caught a cold, it was Becky who made chicken soup and doled out cough drops.

Since Jane's own mother had died giving birth to her, those maternal qualities in Becky had drawn Jane to her. The roommates had always assumed that Becky would have the largest family and find a career that involved children. The scenario would be perfect for her patient, nurturing personality.

Jane popped another almond into her mouth. She couldn't, in fact, remember Becky ever being very upset about anything.

When Jane finally went to bed, she hoped her brain would simply turn off and go to sleep, but she had no such luck. Instead, it whirred with even more thoughts and memories of her old friends and curious questions about what the next day would bring.

Chapter Three

Jane awoke early on Tuesday morning. She showered, then pulled on a pair of jeans and a flowing top and headed for the kitchen. In the hallway, Jane met Louise, who looked crisp and proper as she always did.

"How do you do it, Louise?" Jane asked with a yawn. "Never a hair out of place, never a wrinkle in your clothes."

"I used to love to see you come to the breakfast table when you were a child," Louise said. "A sleepy little whirlwind. You always looked as if, rather than drifting off to sleep, you had simply dropped in your tracks, then woke up and just started moving again, giving no mind to your hair or your clothes. Although we all tried to be firm, you were the funniest little thing. Sometimes it was nearly noon before Alice or I could snare you and put you in the bathtub."

Louise put her hand on Jane's arm. "I don't tell you this nearly often enough, Jane, but I love you. The three of us being back home has been delightful for me."

Louise smiled fondly, and Jane was surprised at

her older sister's uncharacteristic show of emotion. "Living with you and Alice again, here, has made me . . . oh, I don't know . . . younger, maybe."

Jane threw her arms around Louise and kissed her on the cheek. "You'll never be old to me. When I was small, I thought you had to be at least a million years old, but now that's been whittled down to a reasonable amount."

Louise waved her hand across her face in a sign of relief, and they laughed together.

A rapping sound made them turn to stare at each other.

"Is that someone knocking on the front door?" Jane inquired. "At this time of morning?"

They opened the door to see a woman in her early thirties standing there, a suitcase at her feet. She was slender and of medium height, with dark hair and eyes.

"Hello, I was hoping you would have a room available," she said. Her face was flushed and she seemed a bit out of breath. "I know it's early, but I just had to get away."

Louise stepped forward, put her hand on the woman's arm and ushered her inside. Jane picked up the suitcase, which was heavy. She wondered how long their guest was hoping to stay.

"You are *most* welcome here, my dear," Louise said comfortingly. "As it turns out, we have one room free. I'm Louise Smith, and this is my sister Jane Howard."

"I'm Claire. Claire Jenkins."

"Have you come a long way?" Louise walked toward the registration desk and began to check in their new guest.

"Just from Potterston," Claire said, smiling a little guiltily.

Louise tried to conceal her surprise at the fact that her guest lived so nearby. "Jane is about to make breakfast. You can register and freshen up, if you like. Then please join us in the dining room. We'd be happy to treat you to this breakfast. How does that sound?"

"Perfect," Claire said gratefully. "Thank you so much. Just show me what I need to sign."

Sun streamed through the windows as Jane ground coffee beans and filled the coffee pot with cold water. Fortunately, she'd made a breakfast casserole the night before. All she had to do was bake and serve it with sticky buns and fruit.

"Are you making what I think you're making?" Louise asked hopefully as she entered the kitchen and eyed the baking dish on the counter. "My favorite?"

"*One* of your favorites," Jane retorted with a laugh. "It seems to me that you walk in here and say that every morning."

Louise poured the fresh brewed coffee into a carafe that Jane had warmed with hot water. "Can I help it if you're a wonderful cook? Claire's getting settled in her room right now." Louise frowned. "Our new guest is lovely, but she was very distracted as she registered."

"I noticed you took her under your wing immediately."

"Odd, isn't it, how we react to people. I liked her at once. In fact, I almost feel the need to take care of her." Louise put a hand to her cheek. "I'd better get over that right away. Mothering the guests won't go over very well."

"A delicious breakfast is what she needs," Jane said. "When in doubt, feed someone. I'd better get busy."

"I tried to start a conversation with her, but I think I put my foot in my mouth."

"You, Louie? I'm not sure that's possible. You never make a blunder." Jane sliced into a cantaloupe and laid the sections in a pretty blue bowl.

"I saw that she was wearing a wedding ring and made some vague reference to her husband, and it changed her whole demeanor. She was looking around the room, saying how much she loved it. Then I misspoke and she grew very silent."

"Maybe that explains why she came here alone. Something may be awry at home."

"Maybe." Louise shrugged. "She wanted to know if we put chocolates on the pillows every night and if we kept fresh ice water in the pitcher. I think perhaps she's a bit spoiled."

"You don't seem to mind."

"She also seems sweet." Louise watched Jane work for a moment. "I'll go bring the coffee and fruit into the dining room and wait for her there."

Jane was busy at the stove when Louise returned to the kitchen some time later.

"Claire is enjoying her melon," she said. "And Alice has just come downstairs."

"Great. The timing is perfect." Jane bent to pull the pan from the oven and cut a generous piece for Claire and added a gooey sticky bun, then prepared three more plates. She and Louise carried the plates into the dining room where Alice and their guest were waiting.

"How magnificent," Claire murmured. "Surely you didn't do all that for me?"

"Of course I did. When we don't have guests, I make my sisters eat cold cereal. Right, ladies?"

"Don't believe her for a moment." Louise put the plates down carefully. "Enjoy."

Claire picked up her fork, then put it down again and burst into tears.

Jane regarded her with surprise. She had seen a lot of responses to her cooking but she couldn't remember the last time someone had erupted in sobs.

"Are you okay, dear?" Alice asked immediately. "Is something wrong?"

"It . . . it's . . . wonderful. I feel so pampered here."

"That's what we want. But we don't want to make you cry," Jane said.

Claire gave a wobbly smile and rubbed at her eye with the back of her hand. "I'm not usually so emotional, but I didn't sleep much last night. Let's just say I've been a little upset."

The sisters waited, but Claire didn't elaborate. Instead she seemed to shake off for the moment whatever was troubling her and started to eat her breakfast.

"How did you discover Grace Chapel Inn?" Alice asked.

"I've heard from friends how nice it is. My girlfriend spent two or three days here just decompressing after a big project at work." Claire smiled faintly. "I needed a peaceful place that would offer me time to think."

"You've come to the right spot," Louise assured her. "We'll be sure not to disturb you."

"Oh, I don't want to be alone with my thoughts 24/7. I may need someone to talk to." A shadow crossed her pretty features. "I might as well be frank with you. My husband did something that hurt me and I needed to have some space . . ." Her voice trailed away.

"If there is anything we can do, please let us know," Louise said gently.

Claire rose from her chair, "I plan to take you up on that. Thank you so much. I already know I made a good choice coming here. But if you'll excuse me, I think I'll go to my room and lie down. I suddenly feel like taking a nap. The charm of this place must already be working." Blushing slightly, she hurried from the room.

"God's just tossing us people who seem to need us, isn't He?" Jane said wryly.

Alice glanced at her wristwatch. "I'd love to stay and chat but unfortunately I have to go to work. I'd like to spend some time with Claire, too, but I'll have to put that off until later. Jane, have you seen my sweater? Even though it's nearly July, I get chilled in the air-conditioning at the hospital."

Jane pointed to the back of a chair from which Alice's tan sweater hung. "Over there."

"I'll visit with Claire later," Louise offered. "If she wants to talk, that is. You have enough on your plate, Alice. And Jane certainly can't take on any more, not with her friends coming in a few hours. Let me deal with Claire."

"Gladly," Jane and Alice said in unison. Claire was secure in Louise's capable hands.

After breakfast, Jane put together everything she'd need for an easy dinner of red pepper tostadas with sirloin steak, a strawberry and spinach salad and, for a fun and unexpected dessert, caramel apples dipped in chopped pecans, dried cherries and crushed candy bars. She recalled that all three of her friends had been particularly fond of caramel apples in the fall. While autumn was a long way off, this would be a nostalgic surprise for them.

Then, since there was no more preparation to be done for her friends' arrival, Jane took a couple of small packages that had to be mailed from the desk and walked toward the post office.

As usual, her path was not a straight one. She strolled by the Coffee Shop and waved at the patrons enjoying their morning coffee, poked her head in at the Good Apple Bakery to say hello and take a deep whiff of the delicious aroma of baking bread, and then veered off toward Sylvia's Buttons, a fabric and craft shop owned by her good friend Sylvia Songer.

"Hey, lady, what's up?"

Sylvia looked up from the table where she was meticulously cutting fabric for quilt kits that she sold at the store. In a vivid purple smock and appliquéd jeans, she was as bright as the multitude of prints and florals surrounding her. She pushed back a strand of her strawberry blonde hair and smiled.

"Oh good. An excuse to quit cutting for a while. My back is killing me." Sylvia kneaded her lower back and gave a long sigh. "Sometimes I lose track of time, and when I finally remember to take a break, I'm so stiff that I wonder if I'll have to spend the rest of my life bent at an eighty-degree angle."

Jane put an arm around Sylvia's shoulders and gave her a quick hug. "You work too hard."

"That's the pot calling the kettle black," Sylvia

retorted cheerfully. She laid her scissors on top of the material.

Jane moved toward the stacks of cloth. "You truly are an artist, Sylvia. These combinations are fabulous."

"Let's hope my customers think so." She sounded a little wistful.

"Business slow these days?"

"More so than usual. I know it will pick up again, but you know me. I get bored if there's not something to keep me busy."

"Then you should be working for us at the inn," Jane murmured. "It's hopping there right now. One of our guests arrived at just after six this morning."

"Isn't this the day of the big reunion?" Sylvia sat down on a stool behind the counter. Jane pulled up a second stool and faced her.

"Yes. Why don't you come over for dinner tonight and meet my friends?"

"Don't you want to spend time alone with them?"

"Alice and Louise will be there, and Aunt Ethel will probably appear on the doorstep with some minor errand just as I'm taking the food out of the oven. Besides, we haven't been together, not all four of us, at least, in many years. It might be nice to have you there in case we can't think of anything to talk about."

Sylvia burst out laughing. "Four women who can't think of a thing to say? This I've got to see."

"Great. Be at the inn by six thirty."

"Formal attire?"

Jane eyed her friend. "Pick the thread off your clothes."

"It *is* formal then."

"I'd better get going. I'm actually on my way to the post office. Do you have anything you need mailed? As long as I'm going there, I'd be happy to take it with me."

"I have a couple of small boxes." Sylvia flipped the sign from OPEN to CLOSED on the shop window and took off her smock. "A few mail orders. I'll walk with you."

They crossed the street and peeked into the window of Wild Things, the town's flower shop. Craig Tracy, the owner, was inside placing moss into a container. He waved and gestured for them to come in.

"Out for a walk?" Craig dusted off his hands and moved aside a large bucket of long-stemmed roses ready to go into the cooler.

"To as exotic a place as the post office," Sylvia said with a laugh.

"I hear it *is* a bit more exotic there these days. It's been a long time since we had a new postmistress." Craig ran his fingers through his hair, and his cowlick became endearingly unruly.

"Aunt Ethel and Florence think it's thrilling. They're eager to befriend her—for a variety of reasons."

Craig looked curious.

"Well, Acorn Hill doesn't get that many new residents. Even a temporary one is quite fascinating, something—and someone—new to be curious about. And the second reason is really quite sweet." Jane told them what Ethel had shared about the Bible study she and Florence were doing. "She wants to put her faith into action. Granted, she'll think it's a coup to be the first one to get to know the newcomer, but I can't argue with that motivation. I only hope this woman is up to their kindness."

Craig grinned knowingly. "Not to mention that they'll probably get more information from her than they could from Alma."

"What do you mean?"

"Alma has always been quite tight-lipped about the doings in *her* post office. A certified or registered letter is treated like information passed between international spies."

Sylvia giggled. "That's true. Alma has always handled the mail like every piece is marked 'Top Secret.'"

"She always lays the mail face down on the counter when she hands it to you," Craig said. "It probably drives Florence crazy. She seems to feel she has the absolute right to know everything that happens in Acorn Hill."

Jane chuckled. "True. Maybe we should pray for the new postmistress."

Craig smiled and lifted the bucket of roses, then began walking toward the cooler.

"We'd better get going," Sylvia said. "You have a busy afternoon ahead."

She stepped away from the counter, and Jane followed her toward the door.

"Wait, I have something for you." Craig put the roses in the cooler and then reached into another bucket and pulled out two pink Gerbera daisies. "Enjoy."

Jane tucked her flower behind her ear, and Sylvia put hers in the buttonhole of her white blouse.

"What a nice man," Sylvia said as soon as they were out on the street. "I'm glad his business is good. Acorn Hill is fortunate to have him and his store."

As they strolled down Acorn Avenue, Jane told Sylvia about Alice's patient with amnesia.

"No kidding?" Sylvia said as they passed Time for Tea. "I thought that only happened on television and in the movies."

"It happens in real life too."

"And the dog found and saved her? What a great story. It seems as though some major paper should come in and cover this. It might help this woman find out who she is too."

"National coverage might help her find her family even if they aren't from around here," Jane said, nodding. "That's something to think about."

Sylvia gasped. Jane looked at her, but didn't see anything amiss.

"What is it?"

Sylvia pointed down the block. "Is that a *line* forming at the post office?"

"Oh my," Jane said. "And everyone is holding just one letter, I notice. I suppose they all had to write one and bring it here to buy a stamp and mail it just to get a look at the new postmistress."

"People around here need more hobbies," Sylvia muttered under her breath. "They should all take up quilting. That would solve my problem *and* theirs."

The Acorn Hill post office was close and warm, and Jane could smell the faint scent of newsprint and ink. The building had not been modernized in many years and was much like it had been when she was a little girl.

Jane recalled that as a child, holding on to her father's hand as they waited in line to post a letter, she had thought that the little locked mail cubbies contained untold treasures. Right, left, right, her father would turn the knob and she would hear the gear click into place and see the small brass door with its thick peek-a-boo window open. Sometimes he pulled out what seemed like an enormous amount of mail. The scene reminded Jane of clowns tumbling out of a Volkswagen at the circus—just how much could that tiny space hold? Her father would methodically place the letters inside the newspaper that he received from Potterston and then lead her to the window to purchase stamps or, if the woman wasn't busy, to chat with the postmistress behind the grated window.

Jane always hoped that there would be no one else in the post office because when there were no other patrons, the postmistress would rummage in her stamp drawer and magically produce butterscotch disks wrapped in gold cellophane or red-and-white striped peppermints that she handed out to good little girls and boys.

Jane recalled the spittoon, which had sat inside the front door, and the thick sheaf of wanted posters and community announcements on the bulletin board. It had all seemed very exotic and exciting, and she'd longed to learn more about the places from which the letters and packages arrived.

Maybe I had itchy feet even then, she thought. *And it's taken this long for me to realize that Acorn Hill is my favorite place to be.*

This small post office would no doubt be modernized and enlarged as the rural areas around Acorn Hill became more densely populated and the volume of the mail increased, but for now it remained a trip down memory lane for Jane.

A mild-looking woman dressed in a pale blue regulation shirt and navy sweater was behind the counter. She wore no makeup and her faded blonde hair was pulled severely away from her face. A worried crease between her eyebrows punctuated her features.

"She looks like she could use a friend," Sylvia murmured. "I'm glad Ethel and Florence are going to take her under their wings."

"If she can stand their enthusiasm," Jane said. "Being someone's project can be rather tiring." Jane had been Ethel's pet project more than once and knew the pitfalls.

When it was their turn, Sylvia plopped her packages onto the counter. "Priority Mail for these, please."

The woman looked with interest at the return address. "Sylvia's Buttons. You have a very pretty display in your window, I've noticed." She thrust out her hand. "My name is LeAnn."

"LeAnn, I'm Sylvia Songer. It's so nice to meet you. Welcome to Acorn Hill."

"Thank you. It's a very nice town. I'm looking forward to learning all about it." LeAnn smiled. "Nothing like handling everyone's mail to learn about people, you know."

Jane was struck by the odd comment, but her friend didn't seem to notice. Sylvia was still thinking about LeAnn's compliment about her store.

"Are you a quilter?"

"No, but I'd like to be."

"I'm teaching a beginner's class starting next week. You should come."

"I don't have a sewing machine. I'm renting a room while I'm here."

"I have one at the shop you can use on class night, if you like. It's there for demonstrations, so I can't let you take it home with you, but it would help a little. I'm sure we could get a quilt pieced for you while you're here."

"Thank you. I'll consider it. It's difficult to be a stranger in a new place. I appreciate your invitation."

LeAnn would be receptive to Ethel's proffered friendship. She was a regular at the post office—often studying the posters on the walls to see if pictures of any new hard-boiled criminals had arrived. She'd no doubt be even more of a regular now that she'd set her sights on befriending LeAnn.

Chapter Four

The door to the hospital room was partially closed, and through the crack Alice could see that the curtain had been pulled around the bed. Alice tapped softly on the door.

Nothing.

She tapped again, a little more firmly this time. She pushed the door open a bit and murmured, "Hello, anyone home?"

Alice heard the rustle of sheets and took that as enough encouragement to walk in. "Hello, Mary? Are you . . ."

"I'm not Mary," a strangled-sounding voice whispered from the other side of the divider. "I don't know who I am, but I know I'm not Mary."

Alice stepped around the curtain. "I'm sorry to barge in, but I thought you might like some company. I'm a nurse here. We met yesterday." Alice wasn't attending to Mary today, but she wanted to check in on the ailing woman.

"Yes, I remember. I recall everything from the time I woke up with that dog licking my face. You were very kind to me. Thank you." The woman's eyes welled with tears. "I hope I was as kind to others in the past."

Mary was in her midforties, slender, with shoulder-length brown hair. Her eyes, a faded blue, were wary. Alice could see that her body trembled, as if the anxiety she felt couldn't be contained.

"I'm praying that your memory will come back very soon," Alice said gently. "And until then, I just wanted you to know that if there is anything . . . anything," she repeated for emphasis, "that I can do, please let me know."

"Thank you, Alice. And despite what I just said, until I learn my real name, you may call me Mary."

"Fine . . . Mary." Alice sat down on the chair next to the bed.

"When you have time, maybe you could help me get some clothing. All I have are the things I was wearing when I was brought into the hospital and they're in pretty bad shape."

Alice put her hand to the woman's cheek. "Of course I'll find you clothing. I'll bring you some of mine. I think my things might fit, or at least not be too big on you. I also have two sisters. I'll bring some of their garments too so that you can try them on and see what fits you best and what colors are most flattering. I tend to wear rusts, browns and greens. My sister Louise wears a lot of blue and beige, but my sister Jane, well, her closet looks like a rainbow exploded in it."

A smile graced Mary's features, revealing how pretty she could be if the unhappiness was erased. "I guess I talked to the right person."

"I should say so," Alice said emphatically. "God's been pushing me in your direction ever since you were brought into the emergency room, so . . ." Alice spread her hands as if accepting whatever responsibility might be placed in them, "here I am."

" 'Here I am. Send me,' " Mary murmured softly and looked immediately startled by her own words.

"Isaiah 6:8," Alice said. "So you know the Bible?"

"I must." Mary looked at Alice intently. "This is the first thing I've recalled and it's because of you." Tears skated down her cheeks. "Will you help me find myself again?"

Mary's request did something so poignant, so powerful, to Alice's heart that she needed time to regroup.

She laid a hand on Mary's arm. "I'll do all I can. In fact, it's just about time for my lunch break. Let me run to the mall and pick up a few things for you right now. You'll need a gown and robe, slippers, toothpaste . . ."

"I've got this," Mary pulled ruefully on the faded hospital gown she was wearing.

"Well, you aren't going to be in the hospital forever, you know."

Mary looked at Alice, stricken. "But where will I go?"

Alice patted the woman on the arm. "I don't know yet. I know the hospital has a social worker who will probably try to find you temporary housing, but—"

At the sight of Mary's scared face, Alice paused. "But we'll figure it out together. I promise."

Alice was relieved to escape the hospital to go shopping. Where *would* Mary go? She was so alone in the world right now. There was no one to help her.

Except you.

Alice started. It was as if a voice had spoken in her head, a sudden knowing. God. He did that sometimes, making it apparent in which direction she was to go. She'd suspected that God had placed her in this lost, confused woman's life, and now she was sure that Mary was hers to deal with. She would persuade the social worker to let her take Mary home.

"Then I'd better get started," she murmured, and strode purposefully to her car.

When Alice came back from the mall, Mary had another visitor.

"Hello, Kieran," Alice said, her face breaking into a smile. Kieran Morgan lived on the outskirts of Acorn Hill, near Riverton, and though Alice didn't know him well, she'd met him several times. "How's the hero dog?"

"Finn is doing just great," the tall Irishman said, his pale skin turning a little pink. He ran his hand through a shock of red hair. "He's been getting an extra treat at dinner every night, and he sure seems to like that."

Alice laughed, then laid her shopping bags down on the padded chair next to Mary's bed.

"I'd better get going," Kieran said, giving Mary a little salute.

"Thank you so much for coming," Mary said, her voice faltering. "And as for Finn. I . . . I don't know what would have happened if he hadn't found me."

Kieran waved her words away.

"Feel better soon, Mary." Kieran turned, his rubber sole squeaking on the linoleum floor, and walked out into the hallway.

"It was nice of him to visit," Alice said as she moved some of the packages to the foot of Mary's bed. She began to rummage around in the largest shopping bag.

"He's a nice man. I'm so glad I got to meet him," Mary said, watching Alice carefully. "And I hope to meet Finn someday—"

Mary gasped as Alice pulled a soft pink robe from its white tissue paper wrapping.

"Oh, you shouldn't have!" Alice handed it to her, and she put it against her face to feel the velvety fabric. "It's too beautiful."

"Too beautiful for what? You? Hardly." Alice lifted out another box and handed it to Mary. "Here are the matching nightgown and slippers."

Mary opened the package and held up the contents in admiration. The floral gown was fresh and springy and the pink slippers had a matching bloom attached to each toe. "Lovely!" she exclaimed.

"And I stopped at the drugstore." Alice put a large plastic bag on the bed.

She watched as Mary sorted through nail files, polish, facial cleansing products, scented powder, toothbrushes and a variety of other items. Alice had shopped until her basket was nearly overflowing, taking things off the shelves until all Mary's needs were met. Although Alice was always careful with money, she felt strongly that these purchases were necessary.

"How did you know?" Mary asked quietly.

"Know what?"

"That lavender is my favorite scent and that . . ." Mary paused. "How do *I* know it's my favorite scent?"

"It's coming back," Alice said gently. "Be patient, give it time."

Mary sighed and lay back against her pillows. "So now we know I've read the Bible and like lavender. That should get me far in the world."

Alice didn't say it aloud, but she was confident that the Bible would get Mary a lot further than she might imagine.

While they were looking through magazines that Alice had purchased hoping that an image in one of them might spark Mary's memory, a physician strolled in.

"Did you go on a shopping spree, Alice?" Dr. Broadmoor said with a smile, eyeing the packages. "Or have you adopted Mary?"

"A little of both, I suppose." Alice glanced at Mary. "Would you like me to leave so you can visit with the doctor?"

Mary clutched Alice's arm. "Please stay?"

Alice sat down on a chair and tried to stay discreetly out of the way while Dr. Broadmoor looked into Mary's eyes with a light and checked her reflexes. Then he referred to the chart, and a frown creased his brow.

The twenty-third Psalm came into Alice's mind.

The Lord is my shepherd . . . I shall not be in want . . . I will fear no evil for you are with me . . . I will dwell in the house of the Lord forever.

That was the promise Mary had, whether she knew it or not, remembered it or not.

"Anything?" the doctor finally asked.

They both knew what he meant. *Do you remember anything?*

"I've read the Bible and I like the scent of lavender," Mary said quietly. "That's all."

"That's something," he said encouragingly.

"But not enough." She looked at him appraisingly. "And now you're going to tell me that I can't stay in the hospital much longer."

"You are improving rapidly. We have to consider your leaving sooner or later."

A frantic look crossed Mary's face, and Alice could feel Mary's fear. What would it be like to be alone, to have no idea who you are, where you came from or why you were found lying injured by the side of a road? It was almost beyond imagining, Alice thought. It was the stuff of which nightmares are made. How, for instance, had Mary ended up hidden in the grass rather than on the road? A chill passed through Alice. If Mary's injuries had been inflicted *intentionally*, perhaps she was *still* in danger.

Mary clung to Alice's hand after the doctor left, but said nothing. Finally she seemed to doze, and Alice slipped away and went back to her assigned duties. When her shift ended, Alice did not immediately leave for home. She needed to think, so she went to the tiny chapel on the first floor of the hospital. It was a square room scarcely twenty feet wide with three rows of pews on each side of a wide aisle, which led to a small altar. Behind the altar was a painting of Christ feeding lambs. One tiny creature nestled in the crook of His arm.

For a long time, Alice sat in the peaceful silence before pulling her compact Bible from her purse. Mary knew the Bible. What, in here, would speak to her? What was it that God wanted Mary to know? What, Alice wondered, did He want her to know? She flipped it open to one of her favorite verses. "Under his wings you will find refuge; his faithfulness will be your shield" (Psalm 91:4). Alice smiled. It was comforting to remember that as bad as it all seemed God would deal with it. He was Mary's refuge and her shield just as He was for Alice and her sisters. Alice said a prayer for Mary—for her mental, physical and spiritual safety, as well as for a quick return of her memory.

Renewed, Alice replaced her Bible in her purse, tucked her purse under her arm and left the chapel. Then she headed for her car in the parking lot.

She was driving toward Acorn Hill when she impulsively stopped outside the Potterston police station. Feeling a little silly, she went inside. She approached a thickset man in a pair of khakis and a navy jacket that strained across his shoulders.

"I was wondering if I could speak to whoever is working on the 'Jane Doe' case at the hospital."

"The woman with amnesia? I'm Detective Cahill. I've been on that case."

"I'm a nurse at the hospital, and Mary and I have

become friendly. I know this might seem silly of me, but I can't get it out of my mind that she might be in danger from someone."

"It's something we've considered," Detective Cahill said. "We have to deal with the possibility that someone left her injured on the side of the road since no vehicle was found with her."

Alice was relieved that the police were protecting Mary. "I was almost sure you would have considered that scenario, but I thought I should ask, just in case."

"You were right to come." The detective shook Alice's hand. "Thank you."

When Alice returned to her car, she was much consoled and glanced absently at her wristwatch. Was it so late already? Jane's guests would be arriving soon and Alice wanted to help as much as she could so that Jane could enjoy her friends.

She pulled away from the police station and turned her car toward Acorn Hill.

Chapter Five

Louise and Jane were in the living room Tuesday afternoon, awaiting the arrival of Jane's friends.

"You're nervous as a cat," Louise said as Jane flitted from one part of the room to another, straightening things that weren't crooked, dusting off items that were already immaculate and peeking out of the window every few minutes.

"As that cat?" Jane asked with a laugh as she pointed to Wendell, their tabby, who was nearly comatose on the floor. "That cat doesn't seem particularly nervous."

"Wendell is a special case. I'm sure many cats would give the tip of their tails to have it as good as he does. You know perfectly well what I mean."

"I'm excited, not nervous," Jane informed her sister. "It seems as if it's taking forever for my friends to arrive. I thought they'd be here by now. They'd planned to meet and rent a car at the airport."

"Perhaps someone's plane was late," Louise suggested.

"That's possible, I guess." Jane smoothed her long dark hair, which she'd pulled back from her face in an elaborate clip she'd made. She wore trim-fitting jeans and a coral colored silk shirt. She was lovely in a natural, unaffected way.

"Are you concerned that this reunion might be awkward?" Louise asked. "You haven't seen one another for a long time."

Jane considered the question. "No, we've talked and e-mailed for years. Some of us have met for dinner when traveling in other parts of the country. The four of us have just never all been together at once."

"Surely this isn't the first time you've ever tried to meet as a group?"

"No, but Patty was never free when the rest of us

were. She not only runs her own company but she also does much of the painting. There was always an employee crisis or a pressing deadline that couldn't be ignored."

"From your stories, it sounds like you all got along well in school."

Jane stared out the window and over the yard. "Usually, yes, but even though we love one another, there's always been friendly competition among us. It's probably natural with four smart, spirited women in the same field. At one time each of us thought she was going to be the next Picasso or Georgia O'Keefe. It wasn't always art that had us competing, though. Sometimes it was clothes or academics . . . or men."

Louise raised one eyebrow. "Indeed."

Jane laughed at her sister's reaction. "Think of it, Louie. We all had an eye for symmetry and beauty. Is it any wonder that sometimes we liked the same guys? Not everyone can stand up to those standards."

"When you put it that way . . ."

"Although now we've found ourselves, so to speak, when we were younger, we all had big dreams about being the artist who made it to the top, the one who became famous."

"And did any of them reach that goal?"

Jane smiled. "Yes and no. None of us is famous, but we have done well in our chosen fields. Becky, for example, has won several prestigious awards for her illustration of children's books."

"That's impressive."

"She says that it's not a big deal to be able to draw a bunny or a wagon better than anyone else, but she always plays down her accomplishments. I know that established writers *ask* to have Becky work on their books. And the best thing for Becky is knowing that parents and children cuddle together to look at her pictures. It's always been her dream to do something that would make children feel safe and happy."

"She sounds like a lovely person," Louise said, smiling at Jane, who was making another trip to the window.

"I can hardly wait for you to meet her—all of them. They're all interesting. Patty, for example, was recently featured in a national decorating magazine. They recognized her for her faux painting and *trompe l'oeil* business. She works with the most fashionable interior designers and does specialty painting in some amazing homes. Sometimes a decorator will have some pretty fantastic ideas. Not only does Patty have to execute the ideas, but she also has to reassure the nervous home owners that they haven't made any huge, expensive mistakes."

"And you were well known as a chef on the West Coast."

"And now I make breakfasts. Quite a switch from

the art world. Stella, of course, is the most celebrated in that venue. There's no getting around the fact that she is good."

"Well, I hope everything goes as planned and that everyone has a good time. It sounds like the perfect opportunity to renew old friendships."

Lord, I pray that this reunion will be a wonderful one. Bless us with Your presence, Jane petitioned. She now sat on the front porch to await her guests. Her eagerness to see her friends was growing. The conversation with Louise had whetted her excitement even further. She felt just as she had when she was a small girl, waiting for her friends to arrive so her birthday party could begin.

It was probably Becky's fault that they weren't here yet, Jane mused. Becky once said that she'd been late for her own birthday by being nearly two weeks overdue. Her excuse for her tardiness was always that she'd started out behind and still hadn't caught up.

It wasn't long before a white minivan with Pennsylvania rental plates slowly drove up Chapel Road toward the inn. Jane could see the shadows of three faces peering out the windows as they neared.

The inn was an impressive sight from the road, and Jane could imagine the threesome chattering like magpies about it. A three-story Victorian built in the late nineteenth century, the house had a large porch decorated with plants and flowers and many comfortable chairs that beckoned to weary travelers. The colors that they had selected for the inn, cocoa, with eggplant, green and creamy white trim, were historically correct and a delight to the eye. Coming to Grace Chapel Inn was rather like stepping back in time, a feeling the Howard sisters encouraged. What better way to get away than to leave the hustle and bustle of the contemporary world behind for a few days? Many of their guests told them that they'd come for that very reason.

Jane stood up and ran down the path to the curb, her heart beating a little faster in anticipation. The van pulled up to the front of the inn and three doors opened at once to a chorus of gleeful calls.

Becky, wearing a wide-brimmed hat that she held on her head with one hand, exited first. Her pretty round face fairly shone with delight and her wide blue eyes danced. "Jane, this is fabulous!"

She flung herself into Jane's open arms, and they both burst out laughing. "You look as wonderful as ever," Becky said cheerfully. "Why don't you age like the rest of the world?"

Before Jane could respond, Stella, dressed in a lime-green tunic and white linen slacks that had somehow managed to remain unwrinkled during her long trip, spoke up. "What a great place you have. This is something out of a storybook. And the garden, it's perfect. I'm sure that's thanks to you. I remember your trying to grow tomatoes in the bedroom in college. And you had chives and basil on the windowsill." Stella paused for a breath. "Becky's right. You look the same as you did years ago—gorgeous."

"When do we eat?" Patty called. "I'm starved and I've been thinking about your cooking for two days." Patty was wearing blue jeans and a white shirt. Around her neck she wore a red, white and blue scarf. With her blonde hair and dazzling smile, she looked as wholesome and American as the Fourth of July. "Do you still make that weird apple pie recipe?" she asked wistfully. "I love your pie."

"The one she cooks in a paper bag, you mean?" Becky, who was pulling suitcases out of the back, asked. "I thought you were crazy the first time you made it. I was sure you'd burn down the house."

"You're the one who nearly burned down the house," Stella pointed out. "Remember that candle fixation you had?"

"It wasn't a *fixation* exactly."

"You had them all over the house."

"It was a phase. You had a few quirks too, you know. Remember the time . . ."

Jane listened to her friends chatter giddily and a pleasing warmth spread through her. Things hadn't changed much, even after all these years.

"Jane, darling, this is a wonderful idea. I've been looking forward to it for weeks." Stella Leftner threw her arms around Jane's neck and pecked her on the cheek. Stella still wore her signature Gucci scent. She was even thinner than she had been in college and more fit and athletic looking as well. Her arms in her sleeveless silk tunic were shapely in a way that suggested regular workouts, and her makeup was flawless, applied, one could accurately say, by a true artist. Jane noticed that Stella had capped her teeth to hide the small overlap of her two front teeth, which Stella had always hated. After nearly thirty years, Stella actually looked better than she had in college. She was more edgy, however. A tense energy radiated from her.

While Stella was dark, tense and sophisticated, Patty was fair, laid-back and down-to-earth. Her green eyes glistened with unspoken emotion. "I can't believe you did it, Jane. You got us all here at once. I never dreamed it would happen."

"We're all busy, but not that busy." Jane gave Patty an extra squeeze.

Jane might have said more had not Becky taken another turn at hugging her. Her hat fell off her head, revealing luxuriant, wavy, chestnut-colored hair, which always looked slightly unruly.

Dear, sweet Becky looked the role of an illustrator of children's books with her wide-eyed but gentle expression and embracing, comforting manner.

Then Jane looked down and saw something quite remarkable—Becky's shoes, which looked like something Aladdin might wear. The brocade flats with turned-up toes were not the perfect complement to Becky's denim dress.

Becky saw Jane staring at her feet. "Don't you dare say a word. The gentleman at the shoe store said that this look is popular in Europe and very 'cutting edge.' I really do need to get out of my studio more often. I know how to dress bunnies, teddy bears and even penguins, but myself? My son calls me a 'benevolent fashion disaster.'"

"Well, he's wrong. You are a sight for sore eyes."

"You still know how to say all the right things, Jane." Becky said, clearly pleased.

"And how is that son of yours, the oldest boy Blaine? He was the most beautiful baby and toddler I'd ever seen. I suppose he's an old man by now."

Becky's first baby had been quite a novelty for all of them, who considered him their very own real, live doll. Becky had dated the man she would ultimately marry while they were still in art school. Jane, Stella and Patty had been her bridesmaids and less than twelve months after that, hostesses for her baby shower. Jane had only seen her other children in annual Christmas photos.

"He's twenty-seven now."

Jane was surprised not to hear the usual delight in Becky's voice when she talked about one of her children. She sounded almost . . . peeved . . . instead.

"And how are the other kids?"

"Carl, Joy and Sonja are just fine. They have good jobs, and I'm pleased with the lives they've made for themselves. Carl is getting his master's degree. Joy is engaged to be married. And Sonja is teaching first grade. She reads my books to the children."

"And Blaine?"

Becky seemed not to hear Jane. Instead she pulled a particularly unwieldy duffle bag from the vehicle.

All the chatter had brought Louise from the house. After introductions had been made, she helped them remove all the suitcases from the back of the van—enough to outfit six people on an expedition to the North Pole. Most of the luggage seemed to belong to Stella.

"We don't need to stand outside and visit," Jane said. "You can park the van in our lot later on. Louise and I will help you get these things inside. I've got lemonade and iced tea in the refrigerator."

Patty sighed blissfully. "Now I feel like I've come home. Does it get any better than this?"

Laughing, they toted their bags inside but didn't get any farther than the foyer before they forgot about the suitcases and began to ooh and aah about the house.

The front hall was warm and inviting, decorated with gold and cream wallpaper. An impressive staircase in the foyer led to the second floor.

"This place is incredible!" Stella pronounced.

"I'll show you around after we take your luggage to your rooms," Jane said. "Stella, I hadn't realized you'd planned to move in permanently."

"You know how I am, Jane. I'm just never sure what I'm going to want to wear until I know what I feel like, what the weather is, what I'm going to do—"

"Until she goes outside, licks her finger and sticks it in the air to see what direction the wind is blowing," Becky added.

"Reads the barometer and the *Wall Street Journal*—" Patty chimed in.

"And sees if it's going to be a good or a bad hair day—" Becky continued the litany.

"What do you mean? Stella never has a bad hair day," Jane said with a chuckle.

Laughing, Stella held up her hands. "Okay, I can say for sure that you guys haven't changed a bit."

"And neither have you," Becky pointed out.

They all struggled upstairs with the luggage and arrived at the second floor hall.

"This is your room, Stella," Louise said as she opened the door to the Sunset Room. "Jane says you are partial to the Impressionist painters, so we thought you'd enjoy this one." The room had terra cotta colored walls, creamy painted furniture and artfully hung Impressionist prints.

Stella lay a garment bag across the bed and stood, hands on slender hips, in the middle of the room, admiring it.

"It couldn't be better," Stella said, delighted. "You've thought of everything."

"We'll be downstairs when you're ready for that

cool drink," Jane said, giving her friend a hug. "Make yourself at home."

They ushered Becky into the Sunrise Room. She was charmed with the blue walls and bright yellow and white accents.

That left the Garden Room for Patty, who had had a green thumb and loved the floral border and rosewood furniture.

"You couldn't have chosen better for us," Becky told Jane, "but whose room is that?" She pointed toward a closed door.

"We have one more guest. She's in the Symphony Room."

"I'd hoped we'd have the place to ourselves," Stella said, overhearing Jane's comment.

"It's a big place, believe me, you haven't seen the half of it yet. Besides, the other guest will be very quiet, I think."

At that moment, their topic of conversation popped her head out the door of her room to see what was going on. Her hair was tousled and she looked sleepy.

"Did we wake you? I'm sorry," Jane said.

"Don't be. All I've done since I got here is nap. The quiet ambiance of this place is as good as a sedative." Claire gave them a bright smile and disappeared once again into her room.

"She seems nice," Becky observed. "I hope we'll get to visit later."

"Stella's looking good, isn't she?" Patty said.

"No better than you, my dear." Jane took her friend's hand. "Right now I feel like I'm looking at the three most beautiful faces on the planet."

They hugged again and Stella and Becky fell upon them too. Soon they were laughing like the giddy schoolgirls they'd once been.

"You three can settle in and freshen up," Jane instructed. "I'll be downstairs whenever you're ready."

They regrouped later in the dining room around the big mahogany table. Patty, who loved good food and good candy, was already popping Swedish mints into her mouth from the dish on the table and eagerly eyeing the plate of cookies.

They chatted with Louise as they drank iced tea and ate homemade gingersnaps, telling her stories about Jane at school.

". . . She was always the cook," Patty said, still eating mints. "Do you remember the time she spent our grocery money for the month to buy a rib roast and jumbo shrimp?"

"It was the most fabulous meal," Becky said wistfully. "My mouth still waters when I think about it."

"But we were all so sick of Ramen noodles, peanut butter and tuna fish by the end of the month," Stella added, "that Jane wasn't allowed to go shopping alone after that."

"Do you think you ladies could find something

more interesting to talk about than my culinary adventures?" Jane suggested. "How about the time Becky brought home a litter of puppies that were being given away? Do any of you remember how much of our grocery money went to puppy chow before we gave those babies to new owners?"

"Oh, the landlord was upset about that one."

"I really don't know why he should have been," Becky defended. "Our place wasn't all that nice to begin with. Remember the wallpaper? It hadn't been changed since the thirties. There were cabbage roses on my walls so large they gave me nightmares."

"At least you had flowers. Remember the color of my walls?" Patty shuddered. "What do they call that? Bottle green? It was so glaring that I often wished I were color-blind."

"Not a good thing for an artist," Jane said.

"I wonder if that carpet in the living room is still there," Stella said. "It looked like brown and beige worms all tangled together. It never showed any wear—no matter what we did to it, hoping to get rid of it."

"I think it will exist in a landfill somewhere until the end of time," Becky sighed. "Too bad they can't make pantyhose as durable as that ugly thing."

"Decorating aside," Jane said, addressing Louise, "it was a cute little place. The living room ran across the front of the house. The dining room was just behind the living room and led into the kitchen. Our bedrooms were off to one side and we shared the one bathroom."

"There are stories we could tell you about that," Patty said laughing. "Four women and one bath the size of a postage stamp!"

"I liked that place," Becky said. "It was full of good memories. Remember how, when we moved out, we filled all the nail holes in the place with our foundation makeup?"

"But we left the place clean," Stella said. "The landlord said it was 'immaculate.'"

"It should have been. I cleaned the floor registers for the furnace with a toothbrush," Patty recalled.

"*My* toothbrush, if I remember correctly," Becky said. "The least you could have done was warn me before I used it that night."

"You didn't use it," Jane corrected. "You asked us why it smelled like lemons and disinfectant, remember?"

"It was a very close call."

Laughing, Louise dabbed her eyes with a handkerchief. Eventually they all sank into a companionable silence.

The tense lines around Stella's mouth softened, the worry line in Becky's brow relaxed and Patty's uncharacteristic frown lessened.

It was high time they all became reacquainted, Jane mused. No matter how celebrated Stella or

Becky became, no matter how successful Patty's business was, they were still much like the girls they used to be. This reunion was just what the doctor ordered.

Chapter Six

O h, I'm so sorry I'm late, Jane," Alice said as she entered the dining room. "I got delayed by an errand." She smiled at the group around the table. "And who have we here? The famous Stella, Becky and Patty, I presume."

The chatter exploded after Jane made the introductions. The women gathered around Alice as if they had known her forever.

"We've heard so much about you," Stella said after they were seated again. Then her eyes began to twinkle. "Is it all true? That strict big sister stuff?"

"That must have been Louise that Jane was talking about." Alice answered so quickly and with so much assurance that everyone laughed.

"Don't pay any attention to her," Louise advised them, getting into the spirit of things. "I was Jane's favorite sister."

"You were?" Jane and Alice said together, creating even more mirth around the table.

"I don't think you look much like your sisters, Jane," Patty commented. "You are all so different in appearance."

"And in personality, they say," Louise interjected wryly. "Or maybe you haven't noticed."

That comment inspired another round of laughter.

"Alice has something very interesting going on in her life right now," Louise continued. "Alice, tell them about Mary."

For the next twenty minutes, Alice recounted the story of Mary, Finn and the terrifying circumstances in which the woman found herself.

"It concerns me that someone might have intentionally hurt this woman." Alice told the group. "If someone did, and Mary can't remember who injured her, how will she protect herself?"

"You're right," Patty breathed. "How could she?"

"Of course that is only speculation, but I stopped at the Potterston police station on my way home and had a talk with a detective on the case. They'd already thought of the possibility."

"You are really getting into this, aren't you?" Jane commented.

"I suppose, but I feel better now. I was very impressed with the detective I talked to. Even though they're stymied so far, the outlook of the police is optimistic."

"Isn't there something more that they . . . or you . . . can do?" Sympathetic Becky was just as inclined as Alice to pick up a cause or to champion an underdog.

"Trust me, I've been asking myself that, but so far I have no answers."

● ● ●

Shortly after Alice's arrival, Ethel hurried into the house and made a beeline for the dining room, talking all the while.

"Guess who I'm having lunch with tomorrow? The new postmistress! We're going to meet at the Coffee Shop at noon. She seems very personable and open to—" Ethel stopped in midsentence when she became aware of the group around the table.

"And this must be your Aunt Ethel," Stella said, amusement playing on her features.

"Jane's college friends, of course. Welcome to Grace Chapel Inn. Jane has been looking forward to your arrival for days. The inn is lovely, isn't it?"

The guests agreed, and Jane made the necessary introductions.

"Don't let us stop you from telling your nieces whatever it was you were going to say," Patty said. "Treat us like family too. We'd like that very much."

"We almost feel like family already," Becky added. "We've heard so much about all of you from Jane."

Alice and Jane exchanged a glance. Patty and Becky had just given Ethel an open-ended invitation to regale them with gossip from Acorn Hill. Ethel embraced the opportunity.

"I've been worried about that sweet little couple from church—Mr. and Mrs. Billings. He was a friend of my brother Daniel's, you know. I've always wondered how they manage to survive financially. I know they're very careful, good stewards, certainly, but sometimes that's just not enough. Today, when I was in the post office talking to LeAnn, that's our new postmistress, I saw—" Ethel stopped again in midsentence, seemingly thinking better of finishing her statement. "Oh well, maybe I'm overreacting. There just seem to be so many people who need so much."

Becky lifted her fingers to her mouth to hide a smile.

Jane stood up, hoping to divert her aunt's current missionary zeal. "I'm going to start dinner now. If anyone wants to take a catnap or to freshen up, now is the time."

"Sounds good to me," Patty said. "I barely slept last night, thinking about today."

"Me too," Becky echoed. "A shower would feel great."

The guests disappeared upstairs one by one, and when they had all gone to their rooms, Ethel followed Jane, Alice and Louise into the kitchen.

"Brotherly love is such an important thing, don't you think?" Ethel asked no one in particular. "We really should all show more of it." She looked as if she was going to say more, but her eye caught the time on the wall clock.

"So late already? I'd better freshen up too, and come back for dinner." Ethel always assumed she was invited to every event at Grace Chapel

Inn. "You have such lovely friends, Jane. See you later."

She left the room waving backward over her shoulder.

"What do you think that post office business was all about?" Alice asked when Ethel had gone.

"Who knows?" Louise shrugged.

"She has a nose for news," Jane said, tying an apron around her waist. "Sometimes it's just best not to ask what she's up to."

Alice nodded. "What can we do to help you with dinner, dear?"

"The spinach needs to be washed and dried. Then you can prepare the salad. The strawberries are in the refrigerator. Here's the recipe." Jane handed Alice a recipe card. "Oh, and the caramel apples should be put on a tray. I'll start to sauté the steak for tostadas."

"By the way, Jane, have you seen Claire since the ladies checked in?" Louise asked.

"Not since we awakened her from her nap. But she did say she needed time to think," Jane said.

"It always disturbs me when I hear of a marriage in trouble," Louise admitted. "My own marriage was very fulfilling. I wish that for everyone."

"You and Eliot had something special," Alice agreed.

"Maybe I'll just check on her," Louise said.

"I'll stay here and help Jane," Alice said and busied herself with the spinach.

· · ·

Louise mounted the stairs and knocked on Claire's door. "Mrs. Jenkins?"

There was no answer.

Louise inclined her ear toward the heavy wood door and listened.

Inside she heard a faint rustle, so she knocked again.

After a few moments, footsteps crossed the floor and the door opened a crack.

"Yes?" Claire said. Her voice was strong but her eyes were red and watery.

"We don't normally invite inn guests to join us for dinner but tonight is a special occasion," Louise said impulsively. "My sister's college friends have come for a few days, so we're having a little celebration. Would you like to join us?"

"That's lovely of you but I don't want to intrude. You have quite a group here already."

"You wouldn't be intruding. Alice and I are just getting to know Jane's friends ourselves."

"I don't feel much like partying at the moment, but thank you for asking. I packed some things so that I wouldn't have to go out to eat if I didn't feel like it."

"The invitation still stands if you change your mind."

"You are so thoughtful and caring. If only everyone could be that way. I'm sure *you* would never forget . . ." She stopped herself from adding more.

Another impulse came over Louise. She heard herself saying, "If there's anything you'd like to talk about, I'm here."

Claire smiled. "Thank you so much. I'll keep that in mind."

What, Louise wondered, *had happened between Claire and her husband that would send Claire off like this?* Then she shrugged, reminding herself that this brand of curiosity was Aunt Ethel's domain, not her own.

Louise decided to go to her room to freshen up as well and when she returned to the first floor, a party was in full swing.

Stella had changed clothes and was now dressed for dinner in a bright red sheath that showed the angular athleticism of her body. Patty wore a sparkling sweater and had fluffed her hair to its full height. Becky, ever-practical Becky, was still in her traveling clothes.

Ethel had returned. She had changed into an eye-grabbing pink dress, which made quite a fashion statement with her bottle-red hair. She was, as she loved to be, the center of attention.

"Did I tell you about the time Lloyd, my friend Mayor Tynan, had to relocate a family of baby raccoons from the attic of town hall? The city council wanted the janitor to do it but the janitor wanted the police to do it. The police, of course, said it was the job of animal rescue and they couldn't send anyone out until the following Monday. Monday! Can you imagine? And Lloyd was scheduled to give a tour of his office on Monday to some people who worked for the governor." Her cheeks reddened until they were nearly the hue of her hair.

Stella, who obviously thought Ethel was hilarious, wiped her eyes. "What did he do?"

"He had to keep them quiet—the raccoons, I mean, not the officials," Ethel said. "He couldn't have animals scratching around up there. It would never do to have state officials think we had rodents in town hall, so Lloyd took a ladder, got up there and opened a loaf of bread, which he put beside a pan of water, hoping they'd eat and settle down for a nap."

"You're kidding!" Patty practically hooted with glee.

"It worked fairly well, but the guests were a little late in arriving, and the raccoons started to move around before everyone was ready to depart."

"Then what?"

"Lloyd's secretary started playing patriotic tunes on her CD player to drown out the scratching. When the noises got louder, she turned up the music." Ethel chuckled until she started to quiver. "Lloyd said that by the time the officials left, they were all practically marching to the music. Later he got a letter saying that the visiting group had enjoyed Acorn Hill the most of all their stops and they were very impressed with the community's patriotism."

The doorbell rang, but could barely be heard over the din of laughter.

"That must be Sylvia," Jane said.

"Why did she ring the bell?" Louise wondered aloud. "She always just walks right in."

"Her hands might be full," Jane said. "I asked her to bring over some of her sample quilts. I thought everyone might enjoy looking at them. Sylvia is also an artist. Her medium is fabric and thread."

When Jane opened the door, Sylvia's hands were indeed occupied. She carried a large plastic tub into the foyer. She even wore her quilting, an elaborate, meticulously made patchwork jacket in teals, jade green and oranges.

"Sorry I'm late. I got carried away packing my samples for show and tell."

"No problem. Come, meet my friends." One by one, Jane introduced them to Sylvia.

"So you are the amazing person Jane mentions so often," Stella said, grasping Sylvia's hand in both hers. "I'm delighted to meet you."

"You talk about me?" Sylvia looked at Jane in surprise.

"Of course. You're a good part of the reason I've enjoyed Acorn Hill so much since I moved back here. Don't you know that?"

Sylvia flushed pink.

When it was her turn to meet Becky, Sylvia surprised her by saying, "I have to admit that I went to the library and checked out a couple of your books. I'm fascinated by illustrations, and yours are extraordinary."

Now it was Becky's turn to blush. "Thank you for going to the trouble. I'm flattered."

"I looked at them for a long while," Sylvia said. "I could imagine some of your pictures made into patterns for quilts."

Becky's eyes grew wide. "Really? What a wonderful idea. I've often imagined one of my characters re-created as a toy or in a coloring book, but a quilt. Wouldn't that be clever? Do you actually think it's possible?"

"You'd have to enlarge a character or scene in order to make a pattern, but I've done that several times. You'll see some of the things I've made."

Within minutes they were discussing the complexity of transforming one of Becky's illustrations into a quilt pattern, talking as if they'd been friends forever.

Jane sat back and watched the interactions with delight. Sylvia and Becky had their heads together. Stella and Patty were listening with rapt attention to Aunt Ethel telling a story about Jane's father, and Louise and Alice were joining in. This was exactly what she'd hoped the reunion would be.

Some minutes late, Jane announced dinner. "Please sit down, ladies," Jane said, knowing the women would keep talking all evening if she didn't interrupt.

After they were settled around the dining table, Jane turned to Louise. "Would you please lead us in prayer?"

"I'd be delighted." She bowed her silver head. "Dear Heavenly Father, thank you for gathering us here today. Bless our food, our conversation and our fellowship. If there is anyone in this house who can use your curing touch, please administer your healing. I pray that this weekend will be a blessing of friendship and fellowship. And bless Jane as she prepares our food. Amen."

A murmur of *amens* echoed around the table.

As the guests ate their salads, Jane served the tostadas. When she got to Louise, she leaned forward and whispered in her ear. "That wasn't exactly the prayer I expected."

Louise glanced up at her. "It wasn't the prayer I'd planned to pray either. It just came out."

"Well, it was lovely."

"Perhaps I was thinking of Claire."

"I'll go up later and invite her for dessert."

"She may not want to be disturbed."

"Anyone should want to be disturbed for my caramel apples," Jane said cheerfully and continued to serve dinner.

As the food was passed, Ethel, who had been so gregarious before dinner, grew silent, as if her thoughts were miles away.

"You're quiet, Aunt Ethel," Alice observed. "Have you had a busy day?"

Ethel looked up from her salad. "I was just thinking of something else. Did you know that Fred and Vera Humbert's daughter Jean is planning to spend time in Australia?" Ethel asked.

"I had no idea." Louise was curious. "I saw Vera yester-day and she didn't say a thing about that."

"She has a friend there—a *special* friend." Ethel nodded sagely. "I do hope she doesn't decide to move there. It would break Fred and Vera's hearts to have her so far away."

"Vera didn't mention anything about that the last time I spoke with her," Alice said. "I'm sure that she would have told me. Although Jean was with her, so maybe she didn't feel free to talk about it."

"I don't think Vera knows how serious this is," Ethel said primly.

And you do? All three sisters' expressions said. *How?*

Ethel, however, was more interested in imparting gossip than explaining where it came from.

"Oh, to be young again," Stella sighed. "Romance, travel, first love . . ."

"What do you mean 'to be young again'?" Jane spluttered. "You *are* young. We're only as old as we think, I say. I'm not a day over twenty-nine, myself."

Stella looked at her doubtfully. "The mirror doesn't lie, Jane."

"Jane looks great," Patty responded. "And so do you and Becky."

"And you too, Patty," Becky added. "We aren't old. We're just becoming what we once dreamed we would be—especially you, Stella. Your reputation as a watercolorist is growing, your marriage is happy, you look like a model . . ."

Stella stared sadly at Becky as if to say, *Oh, you deluded darling . . .*

"Well, it's true."

It was apparent that Stella didn't agree with her friends' comments, but she didn't say more.

"How is your family, Becky?" Patty inquired, changing the subject. "You've hardly said a thing about them."

Becky shrugged as if she were uninterested in the subject.

"What about Blaine? He's just finishing his master's degree, isn't he?"

Becky nodded shortly.

Sensing it was time for a diversion, Jane slipped out of her chair and quietly mounted the stairs to Claire's room. She rapped on the door.

"Yes?"

"It's Jane Howard. I know you didn't want to have dinner, but I thought you might enjoy having dessert with us. Nothing fancy. Caramel apples, actually. My friends have a particular fondness for them so I made some just to surprise them. Interested?"

The door opened, and the light from a small lamp framed Claire in the doorway.

"Caramel apples? Seriously?" She appeared amused. "I haven't had one of those in years."

"Then it's time. And feel free to tell me if I'm being a pest. We don't want to intrude."

"You aren't. Funny, but if I'm alone, I want company. And if I'm with people, I feel like being alone. I don't quite know what I want these days." Claire studied Jane. "Have you ever been married?"

"Once. It didn't work out the way I'd hoped."

"I'm sorry. I shouldn't have pried, but my husband did something that's troubling me a great deal. That's why I needed to get away." Her eyes flashed and Jane saw in her expression that she didn't like to be crossed. Then Claire smiled a little and her features softened. "Or maybe I just need to drown my sorrows in a caramel apple."

"It's worth a try. Come on."

A smile spread across Louise's face when Jane and Claire walked into the dining room together. She made introductions while Jane presented her playful dessert.

"Well, Jane, you haven't lost your touch," Becky said as she dabbed the corners of her lips with a napkin. "Your cooking is even better than it used to be. This is all so lovely that I think I could stay here forever. Maybe I will. It's better than going back to all the work at home." She sounded very serious when she said it.

"Or perhaps we could take Jane back with us," Patty mused. "Can anyone figure out how to do that?"

"We've been hearing all sorts of stories about Jane and her friends when they were in college," Louise told Claire. "Had I known what my little sister was up to, I might have worried more about her."

"We were practically angels," Jane informed her sister. "Why, even the one time I thought we might have gone too far turned out for the best in the end."

"Whatever do you mean?" Ethel frowned. "The time you 'might have gone too far?'"

Suddenly Becky began to blush to the roots of her hair.

"It started out innocently enough. Becky had broken up with a boyfriend—one we didn't much approve of anyway," Patty said. "And she moped around the house like Eeyore from *Winnie the Pooh*."

"It wasn't *that* bad!" Becky hesitated. "Was it?"

"You actually *said* the words 'Woe is me,' Becky," Stella reminded her. "That's bad. I thought people only said that in B-movies."

"Anyway," Patty picked up the story, "we decided we needed to help her out. You know, give her something to distract her, to cheer her up."

"What was that?" Sylvia asked.

"We thought she needed a new date." Patty flushed. "But maybe we did go a little overboard in getting one for her."

"What did you do?" Alice asked warily.

"We took out a personal ad for her in the local paper," Patty said.

"You didn't!" Alice exclaimed, horrified.

"I'm afraid we did," Jane said with a sigh. "Thinking back on it, it was a crazy idea, but at the time . . ."

"I hope you told any man who called that you weren't interested," Alice said.

"Not exactly." Becky flushed scarlet. "I married one of them instead."

She burst out laughing at Alice and Louise's horrified expressions.

"He called while my conniving roommates were out. They hadn't told me what they'd done, so by the time Jack explained to me where he'd gotten my number and I'd told him who I suspected had put the ad in the paper, we'd had a good laugh. It turned out that his own roommates had dared him to call, and he'd done it just to quiet them." Becky's blue eyes twinkled merrily. "We showed them all, didn't we?"

"You can't believe how scared we were when we heard that someone had actually answered the ad," Patty admitted. "It was a silly lark. We hadn't considered the possible consequences."

"We were even more upset when Becky said she was going to date him. Just to get even with us she made him sound mysterious and creepy. We were terrified for her."

"Served you right," Becky said smugly.

"She didn't tell us that he went to the same school or that they'd discovered his father and Becky's uncle were old friends," Patty said.

"It's a small world," Becky said with a shrug.

"But we didn't know anything about him," Stella said. "And Becky was so mysterious. She was just trying to scare us for what we'd done."

"It worked too. You quit playing tricks on me after that."

"I should hope so." Louise leaned back in her chair. "If I'd known all you were up to Jane, my hair would have turned gray years earlier."

Chapter Seven

Sylvia, may we see the quilts you brought?" Stella asked, settling into the couch in the parlor.

"Sure. I'll get them." Sylvia jumped up and returned with the large container she'd carried from the shop.

While Jane and Alice cleared dishes from the dining room, Louise served coffee to the group in the parlor.

Sylvia took the lid off the container and lifted a folded piece from the top of a mound of fabric.

"Here's a little farmyard scene I did. I based it on a photo a friend sent me."

She unfolded a quilted wall hanging about three feet square and held it up, revealing a charming, primitive rendition of a red barn, white house and a yard filled with chickens, horses and cows.

"This represents my friend's home. I'm going to send it to her for Christmas."

"It's remarkable," Becky breathed. "It reminds me of my grandparents' place in Minnesota."

"And here's a quilt I just finished as a baby gift," she said, reaching into the pile. "I didn't have the time to work on it before the baby was born so I thought I'd take a stab at the baby's portrait. It took forever but it's worth it, don't you think?" She unfurled a soft blanket with a portrait of a baby's face done in various flesh-toned fabrics. The child's bright blue eyes and rosy lips smiled out at them.

"It looks so difficult to make."

"I like the challenge. If she decided to pursue it, this is what Becky's artwork would look like when the quilt was done."

"You *are* an artist," Stella said, "an amazing one. How many people can actually re-create a photo from bits of fabric?"

Claire, who had been quietly sipping coffee, spoke up. "I'd give anything to be able to make something as beautiful as that. It's like a fabric mosaic."

"You ladies flatter me," Sylvia responded modestly. She pulled out samples of some of the things she was currently working on, beautiful compositions of rich greens, deep blues and warm reds.

"I wish I'd taken up a sensible hobby like this when I was young," Becky said, running her hand over the surface of a pastel baby quilt.

"Me too," Patty said. "After that candle phase passed, you got into macramé, remember?"

"She macraméd all sorts of things—hanging plant holders and purses," Jane shook her head in amazement at Becky's productivity, "and even curtains."

"Just one curtain. Granted, it was large, but I thought it looked nice as a divider between the kitchen and dining room."

Patty stirred a sugar cube into her coffee. "Those were the days."

"I have an idea," Stella announced. She turned to Sylvia. "Would you consider working for me? We're going to be here until Monday morning. I'd like to hire you to help us each start a quilt while we're here. Then, even though we can't stay at Grace Chapel Inn permanently, we can take a bit of it home with us, as a memory."

Patty brightened. "That would be fun. Could you, Sylvia?"

Sylvia glanced at Jane who smiled encouragingly. "Well, the shop has been slow lately. I suppose I could have Justine Gilmore watch the store. She's done it before."

"And I want to buy the fabrics for all the quilts," Stella said. "It will be my gift to each one of you." She looked at Claire. "And you too, if you haven't got other plans. I can't think of a more pleasant way to spend the week. It's good to chat and be busy with our hands. A lot of problems can be solved when women share as they work." Stella grinned. "In fact, maybe I'll start a quilting group on Friday nights when I get home. I'll call it Quilt Therapy."

"This all sounds wonderful," Ethel said, "and I wish I could join you, but I have plans with LeAnn. Maybe I'll stop by tomorrow and check on your progress."

She didn't say it, but all three Howard sisters knew enough to add *And eat dinner with you.*

"Please join us, Claire." Louise's eyes were intent.

"But you don't even know me," Claire said, taken aback by the offer. Still, she looked interested. "You ladies are very generous. I could take a lesson or two from you."

"Yes, a *quilting* lesson," Louise said with a laugh. "It's settled then."

"Come to the store tomorrow morning, and we'll start putting together ideas and picking out fabric," Sylvia said. "A quilt retreat—this will be fun."

• • •

"What do you think of Stella's idea to make quilts?" Alice asked Jane later in the evening as they cleared up in the kitchen. Louise sat at the table looking over the registration book for the following week.

"I think it's wonderful." Jane industriously polished the sink. "It's great to see my friends, and they all appear very happy to be here, but they seem to have a lot on their minds. I know them well enough to see the signs. Stella appears to be nervous. Patty is a tad sour when she and Stella are together. Becky . . . well, she's the most puzzling."

"What do you mean?"

"The 'old' Becky would never have made a reference to not wanting to go home to her family, even in jest. Something's bothering her."

"She is older now and has had more life experiences," Alice said gently. "People's personalities do change."

"That's not what I'm talking about. Becky's *spirit* seems heavy. Everyone is putting on a happy face, but I sense that there are lots of things not being said." Jane carefully put her feelings into words. "That's why I like the idea of our quilting together. As Stella said, it's easy to talk and share when one's hands are busy. Once we all relax, the barriers may come down."

"It is also an opportunity for us to get to know

your friends better." Louise paused to look up from what she was doing. "And I think it was lovely that Stella included Claire. I'm glad she agreed to join us."

Jane walked over and hugged her sister. "I think that you have a special fondness for Claire."

"She seems to have the weight of the world on her shoulders right now."

"I know what you mean about that weight on one's shoulders." Alice put away the dish towel she'd been using and took a seat across from Louise. "That's exactly how Mary, the woman at the hospital, looks. Heavily burdened."

"What's going to happen to her, Alice?"

"No one knows. She's recalled a couple of things, like some bits of Scripture, but it's not enough to help her locate her family or discover something about her past."

"If she knows Scripture, maybe she attended a church somewhere. Could you start there?" Jane suggested.

"It's a thought. I'll mention it to Rev. Thompson or Pastor Ley," Louise said. "They have a list of every congregation in the area. They could give that to the police. Perhaps they could send out a photo of Mary to see if anyone recognizes her."

Alice frowned. "On the other hand, she could have come by car from quite a distance."

"God seems to be directing you to help Mary," Louise said. "He knows what He's doing."

"Don't forget about Aunt Ethel. She'll spread the news." Jane joined them at the table.

"If she's not too busy with the poor woman she's determined to befriend," Alice said. Jane laughed, but Louise gave them both a stern look.

"Extra prayers tonight," Louise said, nodding. Her sisters nodded in agreement.

The door to Stella's room was slightly ajar as Jane passed. She stopped and rapped softly.

"Come in," Stella called from the bathroom.

"You didn't even ask who it was."

"It had to be someone I like. Those are the only people here, you know." Stella's face was covered in an aqua facial masque and when she spoke her lips barely moved. She'd pulled her hair back from her face with a terry-cloth band.

"You would scare off a bad guy with that gunk on your face anyway. What's it supposed to do for you?"

"It's drawing out impurities. I've become a bit of a fanatic about my skin. I wish I'd started doing this years ago, before I was a lifeguard and thought of a tan as beautifying, not sun damage." She looked worried even beneath the concealing masque. "There are so many things I wish I'd done differently. Moisturizer, sunblock, organic foods . . ."

"But you're doing all that now." Jane sat down on the bed and made herself at home. "So what's the point of looking back?"

"Hold on a minute. I've got to chip this thing off." Stella disappeared and water began to run in the bathroom. Two minutes later Stella emerged masqueless, with ruddy cheeks.

"Don't you have regrets, Jane?" She picked up the conversation right where they'd left off. "I would look so much better now if I'd listened to my mother. 'Stella, wear a hat in the sun,' 'don't lie on the deck and bake like a pan of cookies . . .' you get the idea."

"You're always hard on yourself."

"You think I'm hard on myself now? You should have known me at fourteen."

"What were you like back then?" Jane took one of Stella's pillows, laid it across her lap and put her elbows on it, propping her chin in her hands, just like she'd done a hundred times when they'd roomed together.

"About forty pounds heavier, for one thing." Stella appeared amused by the startled expression on Jane's face. "That's right. I was a roly-poly teenager."

"It's difficult to believe, looking at you now." Jane cocked her head a bit and studied her friend. "You never mentioned a weight problem."

"It was too close to me back then. I didn't want to talk about it. Later it just didn't seem relevant." Stella curled up on a chair across from Jane. There was no hint of a chubby teenager in the lithe woman of today. "I allowed my feelings about my looks to run my life. In some ways I'm afraid I still do."

"You look fabulous for your age."

Stella groaned. *"For my age*? I don't want to look my age, Jane. I want to look younger."

Stella, with her feet curled under her on the chair, her hair damp and tousled and her face glowing from the cleansing, looked just fine to Jane. "What's this about, Stella? Fighting World War Wrinkle? I've noticed you staring at yourself in the mirrors around the inn."

"Sometimes I still feel like I can't keep up," Stella said softly. "You should see some of the beautiful young women who come through my husband's gallery. Sometimes I don't feel fifty, I feel a *thousand*! I don't like the idea of being an old lady doddering around the edges of this glamorous crowd any more than I enjoyed having the nick-name 'Chub' in junior high."

"You are talented, beautiful and stylish. Who could hope to compete with that—at any age?"

"That's what my husband Al says." She sighed. "He's a wonderful man." Stella began to look at her finely polished finger nails, and her next question was not as casual as she tried to make it sound.

"Have you noticed that when a woman turns fifty she disappears?"

Jane held out her arm and looked at it. Then she waggled her fingers. "Nope. Still here."

"Not literally, of course, but figuratively. People don't *notice* women our age. We become . . . inconsequential."

"It's not other people we need to be noticed by, Stella, it's God, and He's fully aware of our presence."

Stella smiled a little wanly at Jane. "Oh, never mind. You're so unaffected and natural that these types of things never enter your mind."

"And they shouldn't enter yours." Jane stood up and embraced her friend. "If you worried less, you could smile more, and everyone would notice that. But I know that you can't turn off old feelings and memories like a light switch. Just don't let them keep you from recognizing the person you really are."

Stella put her hand on Jane's cheek. "I'm so glad we're here. It does me good to be around someone calm and centered like you."

Jane didn't dispute Stella's statement. While no one was ever "calm and centered" all the time, as long as she stayed close to God, Jane did a better job of keeping on an even keel.

Chapter Eight

Alice hummed along with the radio as she drove toward Potterston Wednesday morning. The day before had been full with the arrival of their guests at the inn, but she didn't feel tired. She was, in fact, invigorated. It was early in the morning, and the sky was growing incrementally lighter as the sun rose in the sky. Dawn was a bit of God's most artistic handiwork, she mused.

She was more eager to get to work today than she had been in a long time, and it wasn't because she had only a four-hour shift this morning. She was brimming with curiosity about how Mary was doing. Had she remembered anything? Had the police discovered something new?

She parked in her usual spot in employee parking and entered the building through a side door. She changed into the practical, heavy-soled shoes she preferred to wear on the unyielding hospital tile floors, ran a comb through her hair and began her day.

Alice was swept into her duties and didn't find time to visit Mary's room until her shift was complete. The door was closed, and she could hear voices inside. Then she heard Mary wail loudly, "But what am I going to do?"

Impulsively, Alice rapped on the door and stepped into the room. One of the physicians on staff was there, his nurse and, to her surprise, Rev. Kenneth Thompson.

Mary turned frightened eyes toward Alice. "Help me. Please." Her external bruises were fading rapidly, but she seemed as wounded as ever on the inside.

Alice looked from the doctor to Rev. Thompson and back to Mary.

"Hello, Alice. Louise passed on the suggestion about faxing area churches with Mary's photo. I did that early this morning, but we've not received any responses yet," Rev. Thompson said. He was, as always, immaculately dressed, wearing a white button-down shirt and a navy blazer with a small gold cross in his lapel. "I asked that they include Mary in their prayer chains."

"The doctor says I'm ready to leave the hospital." Mary's voice quivered. "But I don't have anywhere to go."

"We'll call the social worker and—" the doctor began, but Mary cut him off.

"I don't want a social worker. I want my life back. You're a doctor—do something!"

"Our church, Grace Chapel, has a fund for emergencies. This definitely falls into that category. We can provide you funds for a hotel room and meals," Rev. Thompson said.

Mary turned to Alice. Now there was terror in her eyes.

Alice's heart, which was tender in any circumstance, melted completely. A single verse came into her mind. *"Religion . . . is this: to look after orphans and widows in their distress"*(James 1:27).

"Mary, you'll come home with me," Alice said.

That left them all speechless.

"But you don't know me," Mary finally said. "*I* don't even know me."

"I know you need help. I also know that the Good Samaritan who found the injured man by the side of the road didn't know him either, but he stopped anyway."

What Alice didn't add was that those words of invitation had come out of her mouth practically unbidden. She hadn't had time to think it through and obviously hadn't consulted her sisters. The inn was completely full, and every bed was taken, yet she knew that God was prodding her to help this woman. If God wanted something to happen, He'd help her get it done. All she had to be was obedient.

Mary stared at her puzzled, until Rev. Thompson asked Mary gently, "Do you *know* the story of the Good Samaritan?"

Mary's brow furrowed. "It sounds as though I should know it, but . . ."

Pastor Thompson opened the Bible he was holding to the Gospel of Luke. "In Scripture, a lawyer once asked Jesus whom he might consider his neighbor," Rev. Thompson said. "Jesus told a story about a man beaten and left for dead on the side of the road. Three men walked past him as he lay on the ground. Two moved to the far side of the road but the third stopped to help, bound his wounds and paid an innkeeper to care for him. ' "Which of these three," ' " Pastor Thompson read,

" ' "do you think was a neighbor to the man who fell into the hands of the robbers?" ' " Jesus asked. The lawyer responded, ' "The one who had mercy on him." ' " (Luke 10:36).

Mary stared at Alice. "You'd do that for me?"

"Of course I would. Acorn Hill isn't far from here. You can stay in touch with both the doctor and the police."

"Are you sure you have room? I don't need much space, but taking me into your home . . ."

Alice exchanged a glance with Rev. Thompson. "Let's just say that somehow, I'll find you room at the inn."

It wasn't until Mary was checked out of the hospital and sitting in the waiting room that Alice began to get nervous.

"I hope my sisters won't be upset with me," she said in an aside to Rev. Thompson, who was helping her with the discharge paperwork.

"You three are a household of Good Samaritans." His smile warmed his expression. "I believe they will be glad to help."

"Oh, I have no doubt of that. The problem is that we don't have an empty bed in the place. Every room is occupied. I didn't stop to consider that. The invitation just spilled out. We do have ways of squeezing another person or two into the house, but it means sharing bedrooms."

"If God extended the invitation then He'll find the space for her. And, don't forget, our Helping

103

Hands ministry will help with the cost of Mary's board and room."

"It'll be interesting to see how God works things out this time," Alice said with a worried smile before she motioned for Mary to go with her to the car.

On the way to Acorn Hill, Alice told Mary about her sisters and how they had come together to turn their old childhood home into a bed-and-breakfast. She entertained her with stories about Louise and Jane and how she and Louise had taken on the role of mothering their little sister.

"We tease Jane about giving us gray hairs, but of course it isn't true. Jane is such a blessing, and her talent in the kitchen is a good part of the reason Grace Chapel Inn is so successful."

Mary looked interested, so Alice continued. "Even when she was tiny, Jane had a flair for cooking. One day I was making oatmeal raisin cookies and discovered that the box of raisins was missing. First I blamed Louise for eating them, then went to my father to see if he'd been snacking on them. It wasn't until I found Jane in the sandbox 'cooking' up a storm with sand, dirt, water and my entire box of raisins that I realized that we should channel her talent into something that was more edible."

"I can't tell you how much you've lifted my spirits. My appetite is coming back. Even raisin mud pies sound good to me right now." Mary patted her concave tummy. "It certainly appears I need nutrition."

"You may be a little thin right now, but Jane'll have you back to your normal weight soon."

"I don't know what my normal weight is. Maybe this is it."

The clothes that Mary had worn when they found her were those of a larger woman than the person seated next to Alice. Either Mary was wearing someone else's clothes, or she had lost weight, as well as her memory, in the recent past.

"What are your favorite foods?" Alice asked. "I'm sure my sister will want to know."

"I'm not sure. In the hospital, I didn't like much of anything."

"You aren't the first, nor will you be the last, to say that. Fortunately, Jane's cooking is light-years beyond that of the hospital."

"They served mashed potatoes one night, but they tasted like the inside of a cardboard box. And the peas might have been good, but they'd cooked all the color out of them."

"I don't know what Jane is fixing tonight, but it will be delicious. Her three best friends from her college years are at Grace Chapel Inn for a reunion, and she's going all out for them."

"I wonder if I went to college," Mary said. "It's hard to guess because right now my mind is mostly blank."

"Your memory will come back. You just have to give it time."

"And what if it doesn't?"

"Then we'll cross that bridge. There's no use worrying about something that probably won't happen."

When they arrived at Grace Chapel Inn, Alice hustled Mary through the kitchen and up the stairs to her own bedroom before anyone saw them. Alice heard laughter in the dining room but didn't want to spring Mary upon her sisters while their guests were present. They might be upset that she'd offered shelter at a time when the inn was so busy. Yet, she suspected that they would understand.

"This is a beautiful house," Mary said, awe in her voice, as they walked down the hall to Alice's room.

"It's brought us a lot of joy," Alice said. "God is good. Now I want you to lie down while I go downstairs and tell my sisters that you are here."

"They'll be upset."

"Now why would you say that?"

"Because people don't just drag strays home off the streets. That's what I am, a stray. Maybe I'm dangerous or crazy or a thief. Have you thought of that?"

"Not likely. Rest a few minutes and I'll be back for you."

"Do you have a Bible I could look at while you're gone? I want to read that Samaritan story."

"Of course." Alice retrieved the Bible and opened it to the appropriate chapter in Luke. Handing the book to Mary, she patted her hand and then left the room.

Alice took a deep breath as she marched downstairs resolutely to where her sisters and the guests were visiting.

"Hello, everyone . . ." Alice stared at the dining room table, which was now piled high with fabric and shopping bags.

"We went shopping at Sylvia's Buttons while you were gone and got the materials we'll be needing to begin our quilts. Beautiful, aren't they?" Stella picked up a piece of royal blue fabric with small purple flowers and waved it in the air. "Come see what we've chosen."

Stella's fabric choices were all jewel-toned—sapphire, emerald, ruby, topaz and aquamarine. Becky had chosen pastels and prints with flowers, bunnies, ducks and fish in the patterns.

Patty's colors were a strange mishmash. It was as if she couldn't quite make up her mind what to choose, so she'd chosen a little of everything. The quilt was not unlike what Alice had seen of Patty herself, a seeming conflict of moods.

"Jane, since you are going to help the others, would you set up cutting and ironing stations for us so we aren't tripping over each other? I brought an iron and I know you have one." Sylvia, her strawberry blonde bun sprouting pencils, had to raise her voice to be heard above the noise in the room. "The rest of you will have to be very careful to cut the fabric accurately according to your pattern. No gabbing and forgetting what you're doing now."

Discreetly Alice beckoned Louise and Jane into the kitchen. No one else noticed their leaving.

"What's up?" Jane asked. "Are you planning to sew, or would you like to help the others as I am? You'll have to get your fabric if you're going to join the fun."

"I'm looking forward to quilting lessons with Claire," Louise said.

"Sylvia said today was the best sale day she's had in her shop in weeks," Jane said. "Stella went wild buying gizmos and gadgets for cutting and sewing. We've got rulers, rotary cutters, quilting pins, threads, you name it, Stella bought it. We also borrowed more machines and two tables, one from Aunt Ethel and another from Vera."

Jane paused, finally noticing her sister's silence. "Alice? Is something wrong? You aren't saying a word."

"I have a confession to make. I hope the two of you aren't going to be angry with me."

That got her sisters' full attention.

"Mary, the patient I've been talking about, was released from the hospital today."

"She got her memory back? How wonderful," Louise said.

"No, she didn't, unfortunately, and the doctor said she wasn't a candidate for hospitalization any longer."

"But what will she do?" Jane frowned. "They can't put her out onto the street."

"That's what I said." Alice sounded relieved.

"But they did it anyway?" Louise asked.

"Well, they discharged her. That's why I had to bring her home with me."

Jane did a double take. "What did you say?"

"I brought her to stay with us. What else could I do? She's so fragile right now. She *needs* us."

"Where will we put her?" Louise asked, ever practical. "The inn is packed to its eaves right now. You see what's going on in the other room."

Alice chewed on her lip. "I know, but I thought . . ."

"I'll ask Patty if I can bunk with her tonight. I'd rather enjoy it—for old times' sake," Jane said. "Mary can have my bed. We'll figure out the rest of the week later."

The relief on Alice's face was clear. "You'd do that?"

"You don't do things frivolously, Alice. You were led to do this. We'll try it for tonight. Maybe one of us can stay at Aunt Ethel's tomorrow night if need be. I think Patty and I will enjoy bunking together. We'll work it out."

Alice flung her arms around Jane. "I'd hoped you'd say that."

She turned to Louise. "You don't mind?"

"Of course not," Louise said. "Who am I to second-guess God?"

"Bless you both." Alice placed a kiss on the cheek of each of her sisters. "Maybe Sylvia will take Mary and me to her shop, and I can buy fabric for her and help her make a quilt as well."

Alice's expression radiated determination. "We also have to figure out some way to jog that sleepy memory of hers."

Chapter Nine

P lease don't feel obligated to include me in your party. It's awfully kind of you but . . ." Claire looked at Louise pensively.

"Nonsense." Louise eyed the younger woman. She had brought a selection of Sylvia's fabrics to Claire's room, determined to help the woman. "If I've ever seen anyone in need of a party, it's you." She paused. "Unless all the noise and chatter is too much for you. If you'd like, I can show you how to cut and stitch the top of your quilt right here in your room. I have made a few quilts in my day."

Claire's eyes widened. "You're too kind, but that's not necessary." Her expression hardened for a moment. "I wish everyone were so thoughtful." She ran her hand over the different fabrics, her eyes resting on the darker shades.

Louise sat down in one of the chairs in the room and gestured for Claire to take the other. "Please tell me if I should mind my own business, but I have to ask if there is any way I can help you. We try to treat our guests as family here at Grace Chapel Inn."

Claire stared at the tips of her shoes for a long time. It was almost as though she'd forgotten Louise was there. Then she spoke hesitantly. "I'm not sure anyone can help. Maybe we've blown it already and it's too late."

"Too late? I'm not much of a believer in 'too late.'"

"I don't know about that, especially in relationships," Claire said. "Sometimes they become irreparably broken."

"And you have a relationship like that?"

"I didn't think so until this week." An expression of irritation crossed her features. "I can't believe he forgot."

"Forgot what?"

"My birthday. He knows how important birthdays are to me. While I was growing up, my sister and I looked forward to our birthdays more than any other day of the year. It was 'our' day. Once my parents even rented a pony for my party. The least my own husband could do is give me a *card*, don't you think?"

Louise hid a smile. *All this over a birthday*?

"He forgot the anniversary of our very first date, too, but I forgave him for that. Once I can handle. Twice . . ." Claire lowered her head. "Frankly, he hurt my feelings."

"Did you tell him?"

"Oh, I told him—in the letter I left for him on the kitchen counter." She scowled. "I told him that if he loved me—really loved me—he'd know how important things like this are to me."

"Indeed," Louise said.

"I suppose I've been spoiled. My parents always made sure that every holiday was a celebration—May baskets, little flags on the Fourth of July, that sort of thing—but I'm not asking him to remember Groundhog Day or anything, just my birthday."

Claire drew a deep breath. "Then I got here and had some time to think. Maybe I have been pouting a little, but we're practically newlyweds. Don't you think the least he could have done was remember my birthday? He was so sweet and considerate before the wedding. Do you think that was all an act?" Claire lifted her eyes to look at Louise. "Were you ever married?"

"Oh yes. My husband's name was Eliot. We married one year after I graduated from college."

"Did you meet him there?"

"Yes. He was my music theory teacher. He was a dear man, fifteen years older than I. We had one daughter. Cynthia is thirty-four now." She shook her head in wonderment. "My, how time flies. I can still see her as a little girl. Eliot was so proud of her."

"What happened to him, if I may ask?"

"He died of cancer."

"I'm sorry," Claire said. "That must have been awful. I know how terrible it would be if I lost Ben." She hesitated a moment, as if recognizing the irony in her own words.

Louise ignored the confusion on Claire's face. "It's been several years since I lost him. I think of him every day, but now I recall the good times we had, not the bad ones."

"Tell me about him." Claire leaned forward and flipped through swatches on the bed in front of her.

No one had asked Louise about Eliot in a long time. He had died four years before her father had gone to heaven. It was difficult for Louise to believe she'd been widowed so long.

"When we first married, we lived in Philadelphia. Those were wonderful years. We worked together to restore a nineteenth-century Greek-revival house. Eliot liked the classics in everything, houses as well as music."

"A musician," Claire murmured. "My husband is a carpenter. At least he started out that way. Now he's a contractor and builds homes. That is very different from being a musician."

"Not as different as you might think," Louise said. "Musicians and carpenters both create things with their hands. A musician starts with standard notes and creates a composition. A carpenter starts with wood and nails and creates a home, a cradle or a chair."

"I never thought about it that way," Claire

admitted. "But I think of musicians as sensitive. If Ben were sensitive, he would have remembered something so important to me, don't you think?"

Louise waited quietly, amused by this young woman's annoyance and exasperation over something so trivial, yet knowing that her husband's oversight truly troubled her.

"Did you ever have a problem like this with Eliot?" Claire asked. A quick, wry smile graced her features. "I can't imagine you running off in a snit as I did. Being here, with all of you gracious people, makes me feel a little . . . well . . . ashamed of myself."

Louise pondered for a moment. "Eliot and I did have a similar problem once."

Claire leaned forward, ready to hear Louise's story. Misery, after all, does love company.

"The second year we were married, our anniversary fell on the day his students were supposed to give a concert," Louise said, taking a deep breath. "They'd given many concerts before but this was to be something special. A benefactor was considering donating a lot of money to the music department, and there was pressure on Eliot to make sure that his students made a good impression. I, of course, wasn't the least bit worried about it because I knew with every fiber of my being that Eliot was the finest teacher in the world."

Claire's lips turned up in a smile. "You *were* in

love, weren't you?" She pulled a piece of brown calico out and set it in its own pile.

"Completely." Louise smiled back. "Anyway, while Eliot was fussing over the concert, I was daydreaming about the lovely meal I'd have ready for him when he returned from the college. I certainly was never as good a cook as my sister Jane, but I tried, and I figured I could cook a roast. I set the table with candles and a white linen tablecloth we had gotten for our wedding. I even put on the dress that I wore only on special occasions."

"And what happened?" Claire was smiling along with Louise now, imagining the romantic setting and the effort to which Louise had gone. "Did he love it?"

"My dear, he didn't even *see* it."

"What?" Claire looked horrified, and Louise could imagine how she'd appeared when she'd discovered her husband had overlooked her birthday.

"He came home while I was in the kitchen and went straight upstairs to bed. He had a headache, he told me later, and didn't want to disturb me with his problems. He'd been disappointed in the concert and was sure that the department wouldn't receive the donation."

"What did you do?"

"Unfortunately I hadn't heard him come in so I sat up waiting until nearly midnight. Then I put my overdone roast in the refrigerator, blew out my guttering candles and went to bed. Imagine my shock when I saw him lying there, sound asleep."

"I would have been furious," Claire admitted. "Headache or not, he should have talked to you."

"I agree. And what added insult to injury was that he hadn't recalled for even a moment that it was our anniversary. Worse yet, the next morning he was up and gone before I awakened. He'd left me a note saying that he had an important meeting and that he'd decided to let me sleep." Louise pursed her lips. "That didn't sit very well with me either, I'll tell you."

"That's even worse then having him forget your birthday," Claire said. "Of course, he did have a good excuse." She selected a robin's egg blue swatch and laid it with the brown piece.

"He did, but I didn't quite see it that way at the time. I was so upset that I called my father to talk about it."

Louise smiled at Claire's curious expression. "My father was pastor of Grace Chapel, the church you can see out the window of the inn. What a wise, kind man he was. We—his daughters and the community—still miss him."

"What did he have to say about Eliot's behavior?"

"That was a surprise, I'll tell you." Louise shook her head as she recalled the conversation. "I was sure that my father would take my side."

"He didn't?" Claire looked aghast. "Not that of his own daughter?"

"Oh, he didn't take sides at all. Instead of commiserating with me, my father began to challenge me about my response to Eliot's behavior."

"But you weren't the one who forgot the anniversary," Claire said, flushing in indignation.

"That's true, but my father reminded me that to love like Christ loves us means that *no matter* how someone treats us, it is our responsibility to love them. We aren't supposed to love someone when he is good to us and hate him when he is bad. We are to love him as Jesus loves us—in spite of flaws, mistakes and missteps. We are to respond with the same love Christ gives to us."

Claire looked down at the piles of fabric in front of her. Louise waited silently.

"What did you do when Eliot got home from work?" she finally said.

Emotion played on Louise's face, and her blue eyes seemed to be looking into the past.

"I talked with him about the night before. The poor man had no idea what trouble he'd been in or even that, due to my father's wisdom, he'd gotten out of it. He had been innocently going about his work, absorbed in the duties of the day. In fact, when he realized he'd missed our anniversary, he excused himself to get something out of his bedroom closet. He came back with a lovely gold necklace he'd purchased for the occasion."

"So he hadn't forgotten after all, at least not completely."

Louise smiled with satisfaction. "My father was a very wise man."

Claire was silent for a long time. "You've given me a lot to think about, Louise."

"You're sure this is okay with you?" Jane asked Wednesday night as she and Patty sat on Patty's bed in their pajamas. They'd done this a hundred times as young women, but now that they were adults she was afraid Patty would be less thrilled about sharing her room.

"I think it's great. I have you all to myself." Patty looked pleased about the prospect. "It's hard for me to get a word in edgewise with Stella around."

Jane smiled but didn't say anything.

"Sometimes I just don't know about that woman," Patty said. "I *love* Stella. I just don't like her very much at times. She grates on my nerves."

"Why do you think that is?" Jane leaned back against her pillows and stretched her legs out in front of her.

"The first time I saw Stella she was strolling across a parking lot on campus. All the other students looked pretty normal, but Stella was so . . . exotic. Her dark hair was pulled back from her face, and she wore the most amazing sunglasses. She was about a size two. I could tell, even from a distance, that her purse was a real designer bag. I felt like a big clunky oaf just being near her."

"You? A clunky oaf? What parallel universe were you living in?"

"Stella made me feel inferior from the moment we met," Patty admitted ruefully.

Jane shook her head in disbelief. "Amazing," she murmured.

"What?"

"Here you are, talking about how inferior Stella made you feel. If only you'd heard our conversation earlier, when Stella told me how she'd struggled with self-esteem as a chubby teenager."

"You're kidding, right?" Patty's expressive eyes were doubtful.

"I'm afraid not. You and Stella have more in common than you have differences." Jane told her a little of what she and Stella had discussed.

"I never knew." Patty smoothed the leg of her pajamas with the palm of her hand. "I liked her, of course, when I got to know her. I couldn't help it. She's generous and funny and very kind. It might have been different if we hadn't shared so many art classes. Stella is quick. She's sure of her work and gets right down to business. I'm always second-guessing myself. I just felt like I could never keep up."

"And now?"

"I'm satisfied with what I do. I have a good business. My name isn't on the lips of the art critics, but I do have a lot of decorators who think I can do magic with paint and brushes. It's just that some . . . things . . . have flooded back." Her expression was pained. "And now that I know how mistaken I was, I feel even worse."

"Things?" Jane was quick to pick up on Patty's elusive statement. "What things?"

"Stuff that happened between Stella and me. That's all." Patty's expression darkened. "I was a stupid kid."

"What happened between the two of you that was so important that you'd carry it forward all these years?"

Patty sighed and shifted on the bed. "Remember Barry Handgrove?"

"I do. Cute guy. Nice too. I seem to remember . . ." Jane paused and her eyes widened. "You and Stella had a crush on him at the same time, right?"

"I never had a chance. What guy wouldn't prefer Stella to gangly old me?"

"Several, I imagine."

"Not Barry. He was crazy about her. And I was crazy about him. Not a nice situation to be in."

"Stella liked him a lot, too, I remember."

"Yes. He gave her a necklace with a real diamond in it."

"I recall that. It was an item of gossip for a long time. Everyone thought an engagement ring might be next, but it never happened. There was something about that necklace . . . didn't they break up over it eventually? I can't quite remember."

"The necklace disappeared. Barry was very hurt

and angry. Stella said she was sure she'd put it in her drawer and just didn't know what happened to it. Barry said that if the necklace had really meant something to her, she would have taken better care of it. The argument turned bitter, and they decided not to go with each other anymore."

"But what does that have to do with you and Stella? It happened almost thirty years ago."

"Sometimes it feels like just yesterday that we were in school." Patty looked dreamily into the distance. "Do you ever get that feeling?"

"I suppose so, but I still don't understand what this has to do with you and Stella."

Patty reached for her purse at the foot of the bed and pulled it toward her. She dug in the side pocket for a moment and then pulled out a single fine strand of gold with a diamond dangling from it. "Stella didn't lose the necklace. I took it."

Jane stared at the glittering chain, dumbfounded.

"I was sick with jealousy," Patty said sadly. "I wasn't going to keep it, but I wanted to give her a scare. She didn't notice it was gone right away. I went away for a long weekend with my folks, and when I came back she and Barry had had their big blowup. I didn't dare tell her what happened after that."

"So you kept it?"

"I should have confessed to what I'd done. Maybe Stella and Barry would have made up, married even, but I was scared. I didn't confess. I let it go." Patty stared at the fine gauge necklace and sparkling diamond in her palm. "And it's haunted me ever since."

"You mean that is why you and Stella never seemed to get along as well as the rest of us?"

"She was—is—the living reminder of how stupid I'd been. Instead of being mad at myself, I turned it around in my head and was angry with Stella."

Patty's porcelain skin looked gray beneath her eyes. "I've been able to forget about this necklace for long periods of time, but the memory keeps coming back. This reunion made that whole muddle feel like yesterday. I don't know what to do. I messed up a lot of things for her, Jane. I'm sure she doesn't think about this necklace any-more, but I do. Maybe she and Barry would have married if I'd come clean right away. Her life might have been so different."

She shifted restlessly. "And now you tell me all this about Stella's insecurities. It's just getting worse and worse."

"You could still give it back," Jane said. "Ask for forgiveness and move on. You have been punishing yourself for a lot of years, Patty. And it's kept a wedge in your friendship with Stella. Perhaps we'd have all gotten together more often if it weren't for—"

"I know, I know. I intentionally found excuses not to get together with the rest of you when you tried to meet. We've missed a lot of opportunities to enjoy each other's company as a group. I knew I'd hurt both her and Barry. I was simply a coward. By waiting, I made everything worse."

"I still say give it back." Jane put her hand on Patty's arm. "You'll never feel whole until you do."

"What will she think of me?"

"Perhaps you've underestimated her."

Patty looked unconvinced. "Me? Underestimate Stella? I don't think so."

"We're not kids anymore. Give her some credit."

"I don't know . . . I just don't know."

"Have you prayed about it?"

Patty looked at Jane with an expression filled with pain. "No, I haven't. This guilt makes me feel like God probably doesn't want to talk to me. I guess I've kind of . . . drifted away . . . from Him."

"Patty, He's the *Master* of forgiveness. Don't let this keep the two of you apart."

"Can we change the subject, Jane?"

Disappointed, but knowing more conversation right now wouldn't help, Jane nodded.

They didn't say much more as they slipped into bed.

Jane's mind raced as she lay in the darkness and she wondered if she'd ever get to sleep. She knew Patty wasn't sleeping either.

Finally Patty spoke out of the darkness. "Becky seems different somehow. I've seen her several times in the past few years when she's been traveling through my area. She's usually so lighthearted."

"She's a little more serious and quiet than she used to be." Jane had noticed the change, of course, especially when she'd tried to ask questions about Becky's family.

"She didn't say a lot in the van on the trip over here. Every time Stella or I tried to get her to talk by asking her questions about her family, she'd change the subject. I've never known her not to want to talk about her children." Patty punched her pillow. "Maybe someone else is messed up besides me. Pathetic, isn't it? Grown women who can't manage their own lives?"

"You're managing your lives just fine," Jane said gently. "There are *elements* that are problematic right now, that's all. Everyone's life is like that—ups and downs."

"How do you do it, Jane? How do you manage?"

"I've had help."

"Your sisters?"

"Partly. But these days I leave the heavy lifting to God."

"I miss Him," Patty murmured. "Maybe He'd forgive me if I could only forgive myself."

Chapter Ten

Jane left Patty sleeping soundly on Thursday morning. Dawn was just breaking when she tip-toed downstairs.

She was surprised to see that she was not the first

one up. Mary was sitting at the dining room table, wearing the robe and slippers that Alice had given her.

"Good morning," Jane murmured.

Mary looked up. "I didn't make too much noise, did I?"

"No. I didn't hear you at all. I'm just an early riser." Jane beckoned to her. "Come with me into the kitchen. I'll put on coffee and pour some juice and we can chat."

The kitchen glowed with the first rosy rays of the sun. Flowers from the garden sat on the counter looking as fresh this morning as they had when Jane brought them in the night before. Jane took two glasses from the cupboard and set them on the counter, then she went to the refrigerator for juice.

"How did you sleep?"

"Better than I did in the hospital. For the first time in days, I actually feel rested."

"Excellent. We pride ourselves on comfortable beds and a good night's sleep around here."

"I'm feeling guilty, though. I've ousted you from your bed. I feel terrible that you have to share a room."

"Don't." Jane smiled at Mary. "I should thank you. Patty and I had a wonderful heart-to-heart that we might not have had if we'd been in separate rooms. It's like old times. When we lived together in our little house during college, we would have thought our accommodations last night were luxurious."

"If you're sure . . ."

"Are you hungry?" Jane moved easily around the kitchen, making coffee and setting dishes on the counter.

Mary pondered the question. "I am unless you're going to have tasteless oatmeal, watery juice, egg substitute and cold toast."

Jane laughed. "Will you settle for homemade granola, baked eggs with wild rice and homemade breads and muffins? Of course, if you really *want* egg substitute I do have some in the freezer."

"I'll settle for your menu, thank you." Mary looked pleased. "You ladies are being so kind to me."

"We're treating you like we treat anyone who comes through our door. It's our privilege to have you here."

Mary bowed her head and sipped at the orange juice Jane had handed her.

"I hope that's true," she finally said. "Unfortunately I'm a complete stranger . . . to both you and me."

Jane, who always approached things head on, didn't dance around the topic of Mary's amnesia. "Nothing has come back yet, then?"

"A couple of things. I was reading the Bible last night, and there were some stories that were familiar. And when I went to brush my teeth, I realized that Alice had purchased my brand of toothpaste. That's not much progress, I'm afraid."

"It's only been a few days. Whatever happened must have traumatized you a great deal."

"That's the other thing that worries me. What did happen? If I'd been in a car accident, shouldn't the car have been there? And if someone did this to me and then dumped me . . ." She shuddered. "I just can't think about that."

"Then don't. Take advantage of the time here to rest your mind. Let your body heal. I fully believe that, in time, everything will be revealed."

"How can I ever repay you?" Mary asked, her voice strangled with emotion.

Jane eyed her. "You could start by putting dollops of the batter I mixed up last night into muffin cups. I'll bake them later so that they'll be fresh and hot when the others get up."

Relieved to have something useful to do, Mary nodded eagerly and rose to her feet. She put muffin papers in the bottoms of a pan and then began to spoon the batter into the individual cups.

"It's nice working here with you," Mary said as she rinsed out the bowl and spoon she'd been using. "You have a lovely kitchen."

"We remodeled it before opening the inn. I must say, it's the one time I got everything I asked for. Alice and Louise let me plan it entirely."

The muffins were just going into the oven and the eggs, in individual ramekins, were ready to follow when Alice and Louise entered the kitchen.

"The early birds are already at work, I see," Alice said and yawned. "I heard stirrings in the guest rooms. I'd say everyone will be down for breakfast soon."

"Mary has been helping me. We've decided that in her past, she knew her way around a kitchen. She even mixed up a banana bread batter—from memory."

Alice clapped her hands, delighted.

Mary flushed but looked pleased. "At least now we know that if all else fails, I can get a job in a bakery," she joked.

Patty was first to arrive at the breakfast table. Dressed in jeans and a white T-shirt under a blue chambray blouse, her hair pulled into a tousled knot on the top of her head, she looked ready to get to work. She gave Jane a warning glance that Jane took to mean that their conversation last night was off limits in the light of day.

Jane would never utter a word about Patty's secret to anyone, but she hoped Patty would do the right thing. Confession, Jane knew, was good for the soul.

Stella breezed in next, in a scarlet blouse and black silk trousers. She wore her hair in a French knot held in place with what looked like a pair of black, patent leather chopsticks. The diamond ring on her finger had to be at least three carats, Jane decided. Stella didn't "do" costume jewelry. She was also the only one who'd taken time to put on makeup and jewelry.

"Good morning, all. Did you have a glorious night's sleep? I did. Where do you get your mattresses? I want to take mine home with me. My word, look at the food on this table. Jane strikes again. Hello, Louise, don't you look lovely today. And Alice . . ."

Stella prattled on cheerfully, blissfully ignorant of the miserable look on Patty's face.

"Where's Becky?" Stella finally asked.

"I'll go find her," Jane offered. "Louise, why don't you and Alice lead everyone in a prayer and begin to eat? Becky and I will catch up."

Sun shone on the meticulously polished hallway floor as Jane approached Becky's room. She rapped on the door.

"Just a minute, I'm not ready . . ." The door flew open to reveal Becky, still in her nightgown. "Oh, Jane. Sorry. I couldn't sleep last night, and I was so exhausted that just about the time I should have been getting up, I dozed off." Her blue eyes were red-rimmed from lack of sleep. "Is breakfast ready? I'll pull on some clothes and be right down. I'll shower after breakfast."

"That's a plan," Jane said.

Becky left the door open, disappeared into her bathroom and popped out again dressed in a hot pink velour jogging suit. She plucked ruefully at the waistband.

"Elastic. That's all I brought this trip. I remembered the way you cook and knew I wouldn't be able to fit into anything else on the return trip." She peered into the mirror. "How do I look?"

"Lovely. Pink becomes you."

"I look like an Easter egg, actually, an Easter egg with wrinkles and gray hair."

"You don't have either wrinkles or gray hair."

"Not yet, maybe, but they're coming. I can feel it." She looked in the mirror again. "You and Stella didn't have children and look at you. You aren't all that different from our school days. Me? Bags beneath my eyes, crows' feet. Bags on my crows' feet and crows' feet on my bags . . ."

Jane burst out laughing at Becky's cheerful and entirely fictitious description.

"I've discovered what causes aging, you know."

"And what, pray tell, is that? When this gets out, you'll probably be a wealthy woman." Jane leaned casually against the door jamb and crossed her arms over her chest.

"Children. They're what do it. The cause of gray hair, frown and worry lines and bags beneath the eyes. I'd still look twenty-five if I hadn't had children."

"You adore your children. Even if that notion about the gray hair and wrinkles were true, and it's not, you'd say they're worth it."

"Don't jump to conclusions so quickly, Jane."

Becky said this lightly, but there was a hint of conviction in her voice.

By the time Jane and Becky arrived, Claire was also seated at the table.

Breakfast was a festive affair. How could it be otherwise with the three friends telling every tale they could think of about Jane? They passed around stories as easily as they passed dishes from one to another, and Alice and Louise were in their element, hearing about their much-loved sister.

"I'll never forget the night that the cat walked on Jane's painting," Stella said as she helped herself to a muffin. "That was the most upset I've ever seen her. I felt bad for her, of course, but I still couldn't keep from laughing."

"Fine friend you were," Jane retorted. "It had been my most ambitious project up to then—ruined."

"It wasn't ruined, it was just abstracted, that's all," Stella said.

"I blame you for that, Becky," Jane said. "You're the one who brought the cat home."

Louise and Alice were looking more confused by the moment.

"Slow down, please. What cat?" asked Louise.

"Becky volunteered to cat-sit for a friend without telling any of us," Patty began. "She took it into the bedroom with its litter box. No one was home to tell about the kitten, so she just closed the door, planning to inform us later."

"How was I to know the cat was a Houdini?" Becky asked. "My friend didn't warn me that he could open doors."

"Jane had been working for two weeks on a still-life oil painting that she was supposed to turn in as part of a class project," Stella continued. "She took it off her easel and laid it on the dining room table so that she could work on another piece. Meanwhile, Becky's cat managed to open the door and escape into the other part of the house."

"Imagine how I felt," Jane said, picking up the story, "when I turned around to see a kitten walking across my wet oil painting, his little paws covered with paint. Then, before I could stop him, the little thing *sat down* on the canvas. I thought I'd die."

"She yelled so loudly, she scared the cat. It jumped off the table and left colorful little foot-prints all the way back to the bedroom."

Louise and Alice laughed merrily. Mary and Claire grinned, as much at the way the friends were telling it as the story itself.

No one even noticed that Ethel had come in, until she arrived at Louise's side at the table.

"Good morning, everyone. It sounds as though you all are having a lovely time." Ethel poured a cup of coffee at the sideboard and joined the group at the table.

"I haven't had this much fun in ages," Louise admitted. "I wish you ladies could stay until you've told us all your stories about Jane."

"We'd be here a long time," Stella said cheerfully. "Jane was an entertaining roommate to have."

"Would you like something to eat, Aunt Ethel?" Jane asked.

"Just a muffin, dear. I haven't time for more." Ethel took a seat and accepted the basket of muffins Jane passed to her.

"You're very busy these days," Alice observed. "How was your lunch with the new postmistress?"

Ethel frowned. "Fine, but I was a little disappointed that I wasn't the first to show her hospitality."

"Someone beat you to it?" Jane asked, amused.

"Florence took her a homemade pie." Ethel looked frustrated. "I could have been first, if only I'd thought of it."

"I think it's wonderful that you are both being so welcoming."

"I did so want to be the first . . ."

Jane hoped LeAnn wasn't shy. She couldn't think of anything worse for a shy person than to have her be introduced to society by Florence and Ethel, two whirlwinds.

"What else is new with you, Aunt Ethel? We haven't seen much of you the past couple days," Alice asked.

"Oh, there's nothing new with me, but I have been worried sick about poor Mr. and Mrs. Billings." Ethel lowered her voice conspiratorially.

"LeAnn told me that they've received several letters from the IRS."

"Should she be doing that?" Becky whispered to Jane, who sighed and shrugged. It probably wasn't against the law, but it was an unusual confidence to share.

"They've got financial troubles, I'm sure of it." Ethel shook her head and clucked sympathetically, the picture of concern.

She finished her muffin and pushed away from the table. "I really must go. Do you girls have anything you want mailed?"

After they assured her that they didn't, she left, and Louise, Alice and Jane gathered in the kitchen.

"Aunt Ethel was in top form today. She was such a wealth of information." Jane filled the carafe with more coffee.

"Yes, she was. I do feel bad about the Billingses," Alice said.

"I'm handy with numbers," Louise said. "Perhaps next time I see them I should discreetly offer to help them if they have anything they're concerned about. They were friends of Father's, after all. I remember his telling me what a kind, dear couple he thought they were. I believe he'd like it if he knew we were watching out for them."

"It would be a nice gesture if you can do it tactfully," Jane said.

"Don't worry about that," Alice replied. "Louise is always the soul of tact."

"Well, we don't have any time to worry right now," Jane said as she walked toward the dining room with the coffee. "Sylvia will be here soon to help us start quilting."

Almost as she spoke, Sylvia walked into the house and handed a package to Alice. "Here's what you called for."

"What's that, Alice?" Jane asked.

"I asked Sylvia to bring a quilt kit for Mary."

"We'll do a log cabin pattern," Sylvia announced to the ladies gathered in the dining room after she had greeted them all. "Even though we'll all be cutting our fabrics in the same sized blocks, you will be amazed at how different they will look." She picked up a pattern book. "First I need to tell you about darks and lights. When we make quilt squares, one side of each log cabin quilt block will be composed of the lighter shades of fabric. When we sew the squares together, it will add dimension to our quilt." Sylvia opened the book to a page of pictures. "Like this."

"I'm in over my head already," Patty moaned. "Did I ever tell you I was born with ten thumbs when it comes to sewing?"

"I can't believe that," Sylvia said. "You're an *artist*."

"Maybe you should believe it," Becky said as she picked up her fabric and headed for the kitchen to spread out her project. "The week before the

Founders' Day banquet at college, we all decided we needed new dresses. We were all broke, of course, and Patty had the brilliant idea that we should design and sew our own new outfits."

Stella smiled fondly in Patty's direction. "It was more difficult than you expected, wasn't it?"

Patty turned pink. "I had no idea that my machine was set on a basting stitch."

"The threads holding the skirt to the top of Patty's dress started to snap before we got half way across campus," Jane told her sisters. "It was all we could do to keep the dress from falling apart and dropping off as we walked."

"We borrowed safety pins from everyone we met and kept the thing together through the meal, but Patty had to slip out and go home before the speaker began because she was afraid her dress would disintegrate."

Sylvia waited for the laughter to die down. "I see what you mean. The good news is that if your quilt falls apart, it won't be a public embarrassment." She waggled a finger at Jane. "You're in charge of Patty's sewing machine. Don't let her touch any settings."

Before long, every woman had spread out her work, taking over much of the first floor of the inn.

Jane and Becky shared the kitchen table while they were cutting cloth into squares.

"When I was little I used to consider quilting a rather strange concept," Jane said as they arranged cutting boards and put new blades in the cutters Sylvia had provided. "First, you buy beautiful fabric. Then you cut it into pieces. Next you sew it all back together again. I wondered if it would be easier to make blankets out of the whole pieces of cloth in the first place?"

"That's a little like your saying, let's buy groceries—broccoli, chicken and rice—and cook and eat them each separately rather than making a tasty casserole in which they are all mixed together," Becky said. "It's still good food, but combinations are definitely more interesting." She examined her growing stack of fabric blocks. "If this turns out at all, I think I'll give it to my daughter as a wedding present. That will certainly be a surprise."

"Have you done much planning for the wedding?" Jane asked as she sliced the rotary cutter through one of Becky's fabrics.

"We're getting ideas." Becky began to measure fabric. "I never imagined how complicated it was to plan a wedding. The details are getting to me. That reminds me, I'd like to place an order for your famous truffles as table favors at dinner."

"What are your daughter's favorite flavors? I can make a raspberry truffle that is out of this world. I want it to be my gift to you."

"We couldn't let you do that. It's going to be a big wedding."

"It's my gift to the bride and groom then. I insist."

As they worked, Jane and Becky talked more

about the upcoming wedding, but much of the time they were silent, concentrating on the shapes and patterns that were emerging from the fabric.

Finally Jane worked up the nerve to ask what had been gnawing at her all morning. "What's wrong, Becky? You've had something on your mind ever since you arrived."

Becky looked up, her cheeks pink and eyes bright. "Wrong? Who says anything is wrong?"

"It's written all over your face and in your demeanor. You're dressed like a rainbow," Jane said, gesturing at Becky's outfit of blue denim overalls with a yellow shirt and pink sneakers. Becky laughed good-naturedly. "But you seem down. Every time I've mentioned your children you've diverted the conversation to something else. That's completely unlike you. What's up?"

"Nothing anyone here can do anything about," Becky said, setting down her fabric.

"Would talking about it help?"

Becky sighed. "It's my son Blaine." Tears welled in her eyes. "I'm so disappointed in him, Jane. I just don't understand what he's doing."

Blaine was her oldest son, the one for whom Becky had always had such high hopes.

"What *is* he doing?"

Becky's face reddened. "Nothing. Absolutely nothing. Nada. Zip. Nothing."

"Excuse me?" Jane looked up from her work and turned to Becky, trying to read her face.

"Blaine quit his job, dropped out of graduate school, moved back home and spends twenty hours a day in his basement bedroom watching television, reading books and sleeping."

Jane recalled that Becky's son had been an excellent student, had made the dean's list at college and graduated magna cum laude. When he'd begun a master's degree in history, Becky was incredibly proud. What had happened to *that* Blaine?

"He has no ambition whatsoever. He's made no mention of moving on or getting a job. Instead he borrows money from his siblings, mooches off his dad and me and spends half the night watching infomercials. Jane, I don't think I even know this kid anymore."

"But that's so unlike Blaine . . ." Jane said, unsure of how else to respond.

"It's as though a switch turned off." Becky shrugged. "And the light that was inside Blaine went out."

"Will he talk to you about it?"

"Are you kidding? He communicates in grunts, caveman style. We told him that if he was going to live under our roof, he would have to pay rent. We didn't realize until this past week that he was taking the money out of an account he'd set up to finish school. Now he's depleting the fund that could help him most."

Becky sat down on a stool and put her head into her hands. "It is so frustrating. He absolutely refuses to admit anything is wrong. He says he just doesn't 'feel' like working or going to school right now. He says he needs a 'break.' I'll tell you the truth, Jane, it's his dad and I who need a break—from him."

"What, do you suppose, is he hiding from?"

Becky stared at Jane. " 'Hiding?' "

"A bird who loves to soar doesn't just stop flying, dig a hole, crawl in and begin acting like a mole, you know. Something has to happen to a bird to keep it on the ground." Jane picked up her scissors and lined them up with the pattern.

"Lately I've been too upset and angry to think," Becky admitted. "I was married and had a child when I was his age. I don't understand how he can be content with his life as it is now. I certainly wouldn't be."

"What does he say about it?" The satisfying swish of the scissors cutting through the fabric was comforting.

"He says he's 'on sabbatical.' " Becky rolled her eyes. "A sabbatical from life. I can't believe I raised such a lazy son."

"Who is this about, Becky," Jane asked, raising her eyebrows. "You or him?"

"Him, of course. I want him to be successful and productive and . . . and . . ." Her face reddened. Becky slowly shook her head. "I never believed for a moment that my children would turn out less than perfect. I illustrate children's books, for goodness sake. If anyone knows how to make a world look perfect, it would be me."

"So it's not all Blaine. You're embarrassed by his behavior."

Becky flushed. "When you put it that way . . . yes, and I'm ashamed of being embarrassed. I love Blaine but I dislike his behavior."

There were tears in Becky's eyes. "What happened to that unconditional motherly love I thought I had? Why can't I seem to give it to Blaine now?"

"You are human, after all."

"I feel like I'm walking around with a brick in my stomach. I almost called to tell you that I couldn't come to our get-together. I knew I'd be a wet blanket on the party. As it is, you're the first I've told about this. Now I suppose I've thrown my wet blanket over you too."

Jane smiled and shook her head. "I'm glad you didn't cancel. We'd have been horribly disappointed. Besides, we're just what you need right now, people to cheer you up."

"I do feel better." Becky admitted. "I guess I deluded myself into thinking that if I were a good enough mother, my children wouldn't run into the snags and detours that others do."

"Pretty proud of your mothering capabilities, aren't you?" Jane said softly.

"I am. I'm a good mother. I . . ." Becky hesitated, "and 'pride goes before a fall.' " She leaned back in her chair. "I guess I set myself up for that one, huh?"

Jane hugged her friend. "Blaine isn't a lazy guy. Something must have happened that he's not telling you about."

"You don't think it's just pure laziness like his father does?"

"That's one of the *last* conclusions I'd jump to. Maybe being here with us will give you a new perspective about him."

Becky stood up. "Maybe you're right. I've been stewing about Blaine's behavior until I'm so furious with him that I've lost sight of the amazing person he is. As always, you helped me clear my head."

"Be careful. Once we start sewing these quilts together your head might become all muddled again."

"At least," Becky muttered, "it will be a problem that, with enough time and ingenuity, I'll be able to figure out for myself."

Chapter Eleven

Y ou're all making wonderful progress," Sylvia announced to the women at Grace Chapel Inn as Thursday morning marched toward noon. "I don't believe I've ever had a beginners' class so full of quick studies."

Alice glanced at her watch. "Jane, do you want me to help you start lunch?"

Jane looked up from her work with surprise. The

inn had been turned upside down as she and the others had taken over every available surface for their quilting projects. Stella had the lapel of her blouse covered with pins. Patty had put her hands to her head in frustration so many times that she had mussed her hair until it looked like a blonde cloud around her face. Claire and Mary were sitting side by side, quietly doing their work, but taking in every word that was said. A cozy, convivial atmosphere prevailed.

Wendell, who'd hidden in the study for most of the friends' visit, had come out to play with the thread and fabric scraps decorating the floor. He purred loudly as he batted an empty thread spool around the room.

"It can't be that late already," Jane protested. Then she looked at her watch. "But it *is*. Where did the time go?"

Becky stretched, catlike. She'd been at a sewing machine for the last hour, stitching fabric pieces into blocks. She held up the block she'd just completed. "Isn't it grand? I haven't felt so relaxed in ages."

"I can see why our grandmothers and great-grandmothers used to gather to quilt," Stella said. "Chatting, listening, being busy like we are today. It's nice. A circle of friends."

"But I've dropped the ball," Jane said. "I should have had lunch ready by now. I got so involved I forgot about time."

"Why don't you keep working?" Alice said as she stood up. "Mary and I will take care of lunch today."

"There's plenty of stuff in the refrigerator. You could make—"

Alice interrupted Jane's suggestions. "Mary and I will find something. In fact, I think we should go to town and pick up a few things. Who knows what might be fresh at the Good Apple? And perhaps there is an extra blackberry pie at the Coffee Shop we can buy."

Before Jane could protest, Alice beckoned Mary to follow her. "Besides, it might be good to stretch our legs. What do you think, Mary?"

"I haven't been out in the 'real' world since I lost my memory." Mary stood up to follow Alice. "Maybe something I see will nudge it along."

"It's settled then. Mary and I will forage for food and bring home what we find."

"Don't go to a lot of bother," Becky suggested. "I'm still full to my ears from breakfast."

As Alice and Mary prepared to leave the house, the others returned to what they were doing, and the conversation, which had so far that morning covered everything from the best make of automobile to fertilizing tomato plants turned to books.

"What a fascinating group of women they are," Mary said when they stepped out onto the front porch and into the sunshine. "So diverse and intelligent."

"Did any of the talk jog memories for you?" Alice asked as they started to walk toward the Good Apple.

"Much of it sounded familiar, but there was no *aha* moment for me like the scent of lavender was."

"Keep your eyes and ears open, maybe it will happen again." Alice inhaled a deep breath of fresh summer air, and the two women chatted as they walked the peaceful road into town.

When they turned into the Good Apple, they found Clarissa Cottrell frosting a gigantic wedding cake.

"Somebody over in Potterston ordered this. They must be inviting the entire county to the wedding," she said as she finished a delicate piece of frosting latticework.

"You do beautiful work, Clarissa. What would we do without you?"

"Oh, someone else would decorate cakes. I'm not indispensable." The older woman put a bit of frosting on the cake with a flourish. "But you won't see me leaving any time soon, I don't think."

"Clarissa, forgive my manners. I'd like you to meet my friend Mary."

When she turned to Mary, Alice saw that the woman was staring intently at the cake.

"Nice to meet you, Mary," Clarissa said. "If you'll excuse me just a minute, I have to check something in the oven."

"Is something coming to you, dear?" Alice whispered as Clarissa went into the back of the store.

"I wonder if I'm married," Mary said, her voice wistful. She looked down at her hands. "I don't have a wedding ring." She sighed. "If I am married, why isn't my husband looking for me?"

That question had troubled Alice as well. She simply hugged Mary, then smiled as Clarissa returned and put in her order for some fresh-from-the-oven buns for sandwiches and some dainty sugar cookies for afternoon tea. Thanking Clarissa, they took their purchases and headed toward the Coffee Shop.

"I love it in here," Mary said when they entered the building. She looked at the red faux-leather booths with silver piping. The bakery case was filled with pies, cookies and doughnuts, displayed to entice customers to order something to go with their morning or afternoon coffee. The lunch hour was in progress, and the place smelled of roast beef, mashed potatoes and gravy. Three people were just finishing their coffee and pie, including Vera and her pretty college-aged daughter Jean.

"Let's sit down and have a cup of tea," Alice suggested. "Everyone back at the house is so engrossed in her own project that another few minutes isn't going to matter a bit. It will only take a moment to assemble the sandwiches when we get home. Maybe this place will jog your memory."

Hope Collins came to their table carrying two

menus. "You ladies want lunch? There's some mighty good split pea and ham soup if you're interested."

"Just tea for me. Is all your blackberry pie sold? I'd like to get a whole pie to take back to the house."

"You're in luck, Alice. We made extra today. There are two in the back."

"Good. We'll take one."

"Done." Hope turned to Mary. "Can I get you anything?"

Mary's face screwed up in concentration. "I'd like . . . I'd like . . . a chocolate malt. With plenty of malt powder. Extra thick." She looked at Alice and blushed. "It's a memory worth ruining my appetite for, don't you think?"

"One chocolate malt, coming right up."

Hope turned away and Mary grabbed both of Alice's hands in her own.

"I used to order those all the time as a child, I'm sure of it. Maybe in a little restaurant like this." Mary looked excited. "If I can remember that, I'll remember more."

Mary released Alice's hands and held out her own hand, her thumb and forefinger about an inch apart. "I feel like I'm this close to remembering and then it slips away again. It's so frustrating I could scream." She smiled before Alice could say anything. "Patience is a virtue, right? I remember that too. Apparently it's one virtue I'm going to get to polish before I come through this."

She fingered the silverware in front of her. "I wish I could think of a way to say 'thank you' properly. Not only to you but to Finn and his owner. I've thought a lot about how different things might have been if the dog hadn't found and stayed beside me. It took a while to revive me. If I'd lain there overnight . . ." She shuddered. "That dog is a real hero."

"Maybe we could think of something," Alice offered. "A basket full of bones and doggie chews, perhaps? Surely there is something nice we can do for Finn."

The Coffee Shop gradually emptied, and Hope had just refilled Alice's teacup when Ethel, Florence and LeAnn, in her uniform, entered.

"Hello, ladies," Alice greeted them. Florence and Ethel both had determined smiles on their faces. Alice felt a quick wave of sympathy. She hoped LeAnn had enough stamina to be befriended by these two. "Out for lunch?"

"LeAnn has help today so she could take a few minutes off." They sat down in the booth behind Mary and Alice so that Alice's back was to them.

Alice, intrigued by Mary's idea of saying "thank you" to Finn, began to doodle on a napkin. What would a trophy for a dog look like, anyway? A retriever in a noble pose, head up, appearing to sniff the scent of the air? Or like a big bone? Mary, seeing what Alice was sketching, playfully started to offer suggestions about the dog.

"A fuller tail, I think. And smaller ears. Your dog looks like Bugs Bunny. No, not that small. Now he doesn't appear to have ears at all."

Distracted by the sketching, at first Alice paid no attention to the booth behind theirs. Then, almost subconsciously, she caught the drift of the conversation behind her.

"More letters from Australia? You don't say. Someone is very interested in Jean down there on the other side of the world."

"I was in the post office this morning when Mr. Billings picked up his mail," Florence said to LeAnn. "Poor man dropped it all over the floor in the foyer, so I helped him pick it up. It looked as though he had some very important letters." Florence lowered her voice. *"From the government."*

"Oh yes, he gets a lot of that, I've noticed," LeAnn said. "I try to remember the types of mail people get. Sometimes it tells me a lot about them, especially the catalogs they receive. For example, there's a gentleman in town who gets only catalogs containing sports equipment. His magazines are about sports too."

"Really?" Ethel sounded interested.

"Oh yes. Of course Mrs. Ley, the pastor's wife, gets lovely magazines. Inspirational ones. And there's a lady with new twins that always has baby magazines coming in the mail . . ."

"I noticed that Clarissa Cottrell had a magazine

from a retirement community on the counter in the bakery the other day," Florence said, obviously fishing for more information.

"She gets a lot of those. All from the same place." She laughed. "They must really want her to move there."

Now Alice was listening more closely. Her aunt and Florence were grilling poor LeAnn. She glanced at Mary, who looked questioningly at the clock.

Reluctantly, Alice scooted herself out of the booth. She was more than curious about what else the pair would squeeze out of LeAnn.

As she paid the bill, she heard Florence's voice float to the front of the room. "South America? What on earth kind of business does Wilhelm have in *South America*?"

"Did you overhear the conversation going on behind us?" Alice asked Mary, as they walked into the bright sunlight.

"They are very curious, aren't they?"

"That is the understatement of the year. Where gossip is concerned, Florence and Ethel can be like sharks when there's blood in the water."

"The postmistress appears able to take care of herself." Mary giggled. "I hope I have a relative like your aunt. She must make life interesting."

Alice considered what she'd overheard for a moment. "It's probably all harmless. I know that Ethel and Florence are simply intent on befriending the woman. How they do it is their business."

"You befriended me, and I'll never be able to express how much I appreciate it," Mary said as they walked down the street. The sun shining on the picturesque buildings made Acorn Hill look like a postcard or magazine ad for the idyllic life.

She looked at her watch. "I think we'll just walk by Craig Tracy's shop before we head home. I know you'd enjoy seeing it."

Craig was whistling as he put together eight elaborate floral centerpieces. When Alice and Mary came in he glanced up and smiled. "Hello, ladies. What can I do for you today?"

"I wanted to show your shop to my friend here, Mary." Alice closed the door softly behind them.

"Well, I'm glad you stopped by. It's nice to meet you, Mary." Craig slipped a red tulip into the vase and leaned back to take an appraising look. "I'm afraid the shop is a bit of a mess right now. I'm working on a very large order for a wedding."

"Those arrangements are beautiful. I love tulips," Mary murmured.

She and Alice exchanged a glance. One more memory in place.

"You must be helping to prepare for the same wedding in Potterston for which Clarissa at the Good Apple is decorating a cake." Alice leaned in to smell the fragrant bouquet.

"One and the same." He looked pleased. "I've been getting very good business from weddings lately. Word must be getting out about my work."

151

"You know Clarissa well, don't you?" Alice watched him carefully.

"We've consulted on a lot of weddings, if that's what you mean." Craig nodded. "Sometimes brides want real flowers on their cakes."

"You don't think she's considering retiring, do you?"

"No. She's never even hinted at that." Craig laid down a flower on the counter. "Why, has she said something to you?"

"Just the opposite, actually. But I overheard something in the Coffee Shop that made me wonder."

"Well, you know, sometimes people talk without having all the facts." He stepped back to look at what he was doing. Alice watched Craig work, while Mary peered into the refrigerated cases.

"Craig, you and Wilhelm Wood are friends." Her voice went up a little at the end, making her statement sound more like a question.

Craig nodded.

"Has he mentioned going to South America to you?"

Craig looked surprised. "Wilhelm travels a lot, but he's never mentioned South America."

Alice and Mary exchanged a glance as they headed for the door.

Craig put a perfect yellow tulip and some baby's breath in a piece of green florist tissue and handed it to Mary. "There you are. My welcoming gift. Enjoy."

"Oh, thank you, Craig," Mary said, her face lighting up.

"You ladies have a nice day."

They waved, then stepped onto Hill Street.

"I'm going to make an easy lunch," Alice said on the way home. "There's sliced turkey in the refrigerator, which will go nicely with the multigrain buns we bought. We'll make sandwiches and have blackberry pie. Jane no doubt has a big supper planned, so something quick and simple will be just right."

"I'm full from that malted milk, but it was worth it," Mary said as they strolled down Acorn Avenue. "Memories are swirling beneath the surface, and something I try will make them pop into view, I just know it. Thank you for taking me out today." Mary stopped and looked at Alice with true gratitude in her eyes. "Now that I remember malt shops and tulips, it gives me hope that the rest will return as well."

"Time, patience and prayer," Alice said. "That's my prescription for your healing."

When they returned to Grace Chapel Inn, everyone was sitting on the front porch. Small, brightly colored quilt tops were hung over the porch rail like cheerful flags.

"What's this?" Alice asked. "I thought you'd all be inside working your fingers to the bone, and here you are. Don't tell me that all the quilts are done."

"These aren't quite finished, but they looked so pretty I thought we'd sit outside and enjoy them," Jane said. "Claire is still inside sewing. She'll have hers completed soon. She's been sewing while the rest of us talked."

Mary squirmed beside Alice. "I've been thinking. You've got all these guests. Maybe I should find another—"

"Nonsense!" Louise looked appalled. "We wouldn't think of it."

"Are you absolutely sure?"

"The least you can do is let us try to help you settle the mystery of your identity," Alice teased gently.

Mary laughed. "So I'd be like a parlor game? That might be fun. Maybe I'm a millionaire, and when we discover that, I can take you all on a cruise in the Mediterranean."

"I'd like the Caribbean better," Jane said.

"I vote for a trip to Hawaii myself," Louise said primly. "I've always wanted to go there."

"Mexico for me," Alice added. "I can hardly wait."

"Sylvia and I are taking Stella, Patty and Becky to Fairy Pond," Jane announced after lunch. "Anyone else want to go along?" She looked around the room. "No takers? Off we go then."

After they'd left, the house grew very quiet. Alice and Mary took advantage of the unused machines and began to sew.

Claire approached Louise cautiously.

"Is everything okay?" Louise asked.

"More 'okay' than it was when I first came here," Claire admitted. "I was so angry and upset that I never thought I'd ever laugh again, and now I've laughed dozens of times already. This is a healing place." She sighed. "My husband Ben calls me a 'drama queen.'" She shifted from foot to foot. "I hope you don't mind my asking you something."

"Please do."

"I've been thinking a lot about our last conversation, the one about my husband."

Louise nodded. "Let's go into the sunroom where we can talk privately."

Claire followed Louise into the room, and they seated themselves in the comfortable chairs. Wendell, who was sleeping in a bright patch of sun, opened one eye, blinked and closed it again.

"I came here feeling so . . . so . . . righteous. I was sure I was the one who was wronged and that my husband was an inconsiderate jerk."

Louise's eyes widened a bit but she didn't speak.

"Then I met Mary, you and your sisters and it was like a splash of cold water in my face. As I've been with all of you, I've begun to realize that I came here thinking I was the center of the universe, that everything had to revolve around me. Ben was in trouble because he didn't live up to my expectations."

Her expression turned thoughtful. "I suppose, if I'd wanted a birthday card so badly, I could have reminded him or dropped a hint or two. He's a hard worker. It shouldn't be such a surprise to me that it slipped his mind. He even for-got his *own* birthday once while we were dating." She looked contrite. "But I conveniently forgot all about that."

Louise sat quietly, waiting for her to go on.

"My older brother tells me I was a spoiled child and haven't outgrown it yet. For the first time in my life, I've begun to wonder if there might be some truth to that."

Claire squirmed, misery written on her face. "I started listening to and thinking about Mary. Suddenly not only did my little problem seem like just that—a *little* problem—but it's embar-rassing that I made such a mountain out of a mole-hill. The poor woman has no memory, no money, no idea where her family is and no way of knowing when her memory will come back. And I'm upset with my husband over a *birthday card*." She rolled her eyes. "What a baby I've been."

"What made you fall in love with Ben in the first place?" Louise asked gently.

Claire looked startled. Her brow furrowed in thought. "Well, he's very handsome. At least *I* think so. He has a beautiful smile."

"What else made you love him?"

"He's so funny, always joking around. I'm too serious much of the time, and he makes me laugh. Sometimes I think he'd forget his own head if it weren't attached. I call him my Absentminded Professor . . ." A light dawned in her eyes. "And now I'm angry with him for the very thing that made me fall in love with him." She put the heel of her hand to her forehead.

Louise smiled.

"If you don't mind, I'm going to my room to think. I only hope I haven't messed up things too badly. I need to apologize to my husband." She put her arms around Louise and gave her a quick hug before disappearing up the stairs.

Chapter Twelve

I can't remember feeling this relaxed in an eon," Stella said as they walked toward Fairy Pond.

"'An eon'? That covers a lot of years and territory." Becky picked up a broken branch to use as a walking stick.

"Okay, maybe not 'an eon,'" Stella said, laughing, "but the times have been rare. It's not easy to control the entire world, you know." She let out a slow breath.

Patty raised her eyebrows.

"I know I can be bossy," Stella said, looking at her friends. "I must have been impossible to live with in school."

"It was difficult sometimes," Becky admitted. "I never felt as if I lived up to your expectations."

Stella grabbed Becky's hand. "I was always envious of the fact that you were all so much at ease in your own skin. I wasn't. Being a perfectionist was my way of trying to get comfortable."

They were all quiet after that as they hiked toward the pond. Stella had just unveiled a portion of herself they'd never seen before.

"Thank you for telling us that," Jane murmured finally. "I know it isn't easy for a perfectionist to admit a flaw."

When they reached the pond, Stella stood by the water, her head tipped back, sunshine caressing her face. The innumerable shades of green that surrounded the pond shimmered in the light. "This is beautiful."

Patty sat down on a log, broke off a wide blade of grass, held it between her thumbs and tried to make a whistling sound through it.

"What a wonderful place it would be to capture in a painting," Becky added. "Look at the frogs over here!" She squatted close to the ground to get eye to eye with one. "I have a manuscript about frogs to illustrate soon. I think I'll sketch some of these big guys. I can see it already. Watercolors, I think. Pale green ferns, translucent blue water in the pond, these guys on the bank, on a log . . ."

Becky had transported herself from the real Fairy Pond into an imaginary one. "Water lilies, birds . . .

what kind of birds are native to this place, Jane?" She looked up to see her friends laughing.

Becky stood up and dusted off her hands. "Did I go into illustrator zone there? I couldn't help it. This is such a beautiful place."

"I come here a lot," Jane acknowledged. "It's so peaceful. Sylvia comes here a lot too." Jane turned to her. "Don't you?"

"Love it," Sylvia agreed. "I once designed a quilt based on what I've seen here. I used batiks mostly, and made my own rendition of Fairy Pond. It won first place at a local fair."

"And I see Wilhelm Wood, who owns the tea shop, here occasionally. He likes solitude some-times, and this is the perfect place for that. I also run into Craig Tracy out here. He's a student of plant life, of course, and lately he's been taking photos. He told me once that his first dream was to become a florist and his second was to be a photographer."

"Oh, thanks for reminding me. I've got my digital camera in my pocket." Becky pulled out a camera no bigger than a deck of cards. "I'll take photos so I can paint at home. I'll e-mail them to all of you."

She squatted down near the water in an attempt to get a portrait of a frog. Her brow was unlined and her expression relaxed. For the moment, at least, she'd forgotten to worry about Blaine.

Patty still sat on the log, making faint whistling

sounds through her blade of grass. She looked up as Jane watched her.

"Old trick my daddy taught me."

"I never knew much about your parents. You didn't talk about them a lot when we lived together."

Patty shrugged. "Not much to say. They were quiet people, at least at the age they had me." She smiled at Jane's curious look.

"I was born when they were in their forties. I was pampered and protected, as you might imagine. My parents would have been happy if I hadn't dated a boy or driven a car until I was forty-five years old."

She picked up a stick and stirred it in the dirt. "I think that's part of why I married my husband. He's older than I am, you know. I was always comfortable with people not my own age. We are the product of our upbringings, aren't we?"

"I'm certainly beginning to see that in our little group."

"I know I am," Becky said. "My father left when I was a baby. I always vowed to have a *whole* family, a perfect one, because mine was so fragmented." She looked dreamily over the pond. "When I was young I was sure I was going to have sixteen children."

Patty nearly choked on her blade of grass. "Sixteen?"

"If I remember correctly, when you were young you couldn't even handle two," Jane said.

Recollection dawned in Becky's eyes. "I'd almost forgotten. You're talking about the time my cousin's children came to stay with us for the weekend."

"Came to take us apart from limb to limb, you mean." Stella perched on a tree stump, sunning herself. "Those were the most undisciplined children I've ever seen. To this day I believe they are the reason I never had children of my own."

"You just weren't accustomed to kids, that's all," Becky said weakly, a smile playing at the corners of her lips.

"Not all children lock themselves in the bathroom for two hours and use *other people's* makeup," Stella said.

"It washed off."

"And I had to replace everything I owned," Stella grumbled. "I never did find another tube of *Radiant Rose* lipstick. It was discontinued."

"They were cute, though, weren't they?" Becky asked. "Connie and Bonnie. They are all grown up now and have children of their own."

"I hope their children wet the bed," Stella said, "like Connie and Bonnie did mine."

Jane and Patty, sitting side by side on the downed tree, burst out laughing. "You did get the raw end of that deal, Stella, but those kids hung on you like burrs on a dog. They adored you."

"Remember how they answered the door and told my date to go away, that I didn't like him anymore?

It took a lot of talking to convince him that the girls hadn't heard that from me."

Stella rose from the stump and stretched. "Who wants to walk to the other side of the pond?"

Sylvia and Becky stood up. Jane and Patty stayed where they were.

"We'll look for more amphibians for Becky," Sylvia said as they wandered off.

Jane waited until they were out of earshot to say to Patty, "You look like you have something serious on your mind."

"I've been thinking about our conversation last night, Jane. I'm going to be miserable no matter what I do. If I don't give the necklace back, I won't forgive myself, but if I do, I don't know what kind of fireworks I'll set a match to."

"Are you so sure there'll be fireworks?"

Patty's lips turned down at the corners. "I don't want to be the one to break up the old gang, especially now that we've all reconnected and are having so much fun. I've *missed* you guys."

"You've certainly made up your mind about Stella's response."

"I ruined her relationship, and even though I never meant to actually steal the necklace, I did choose not to give it back. After all this time I've finally begun to understand Stella. I don't want her furious with me now."

"How do you know that she will be?"

"I just know . . ." Patty's jaw set stubbornly.

"When did you become a mind reader?" Jane chided.

Patty started to reply, but their attention was diverted by someone crashing noisily through the trees.

Craig Tracy erupted into the clearing, red faced and puffing. He had a walking stick in his hand and looked ready to use it as a machete. He looked surprised to see them in the clearing.

"I didn't know anyone was out here. Sorry. I made a lot of noise and probably frightened all the birds away."

"You were thrashing along, that's for sure," Jane said, "but you didn't frighten the frogs, and that's our primary focus at the moment."

Craig looked puzzled.

Jane gestured toward the opposite side of the pond where the other group was walking. "My friend Becky is going to use Fairy Pond's frogs as models for the next children's book she illustrates."

"Oh, I see." Craig looked pleased. "It's high time Fairy Pond was immortalized."

"Craig, this is Patty, another of my roommates from college. We're here to enjoy the serenity of the pond and to work up an appetite for dinner. What brings you here?"

"Nice to meet you, Patty. Jane has been telling me all about her college friends. To answer your question, Jane, I'm walking off my embarrassment mostly. I had the craziest thing happen to me today."

"We're all ears. Tell us what happened."

He took off his sunglasses and shook his head. "Your Aunt Ethel came into the shop today looking for a plant to give to the new postmistress. She said she wanted her to have it so that when she saw it on her window ledge, she would be reminded that she has friends in Acorn Hill."

"That's sweet," Patty commented.

Craig continued. "Ethel was full of news, as usual. She surprised me by telling me that Carmen Olander was expecting a baby. She said she'd overheard it at the post office. She was delighted because she said she'd wondered if Carmen would ever take time away from the horses she raises to start a family."

"My aunt concerns herself with a lot of things that aren't her business," Jane said.

"It wasn't even twenty minutes later that Carmen walked into my shop and asked for a mixed bouquet to give to her neighbor. She looked around the shop while I put it together. When she paid for the flowers, I handed her a rose."

"That was thoughtful of you," Jane said.

"When Carmen asked me what it was for, I said 'I hear congratulations are in order. There's going to be a new baby.' I told her how pleased I was for her and her husband."

Craig reddened. "Imagine how I felt when Carmen told me that she wasn't going to have a baby but that her new mare was going to have a colt!"

Patty covered her mouth with her hand, but Jane burst out laughing.

"It was a completely innocent mistake," Craig blurted, "but I can't remember the last time I've been so embarrassed."

"I'm sorry I'm laughing," Jane said as she wiped her eyes, "but you have to admit it's funny."

"Not so funny if you are the one putting your foot in your mouth." Craig looked grim. "You'd better tell your aunt Ethel to get her facts straight, Jane. Granted, all that happened was that Carmen and I had a good laugh, but what if Carmen was trying to have a baby and was sensitive about the subject?"

Jane had a sinking feeling in the pit of her stomach. Ethel would feel awful about embarrassing Craig. She would never intentionally hurt a fly. Unfortunately putting a curb on Ethel's gossip was a little like herding cats—nearly impossible.

"I'll wait for the right moment to mention it to her. Maybe if I tell her what happened without making a big deal of it, she'll get the idea."

"Thanks, Jane." Craig smiled at the women. "At least I feel a *little* better now."

"Don't beat up any more trees with your walking stick on the way out," Jane suggested pleasantly.

"No. I won't." Craig nodded to Patty. "Nice to meet you." He took a few steps and disappeared into the woods in the direction of Acorn Hill.

"I'd almost forgotten how small town life could

be," Patty said. "But I think you made him feel better."

The others came into sight as they rounded a stand of trees. Becky waved her digital camera over her head. "I got some great photos. Just wait until you see them."

On the way home from Fairy Pond, the group took a detour to Time for Tea.

"What a darling shop." Patty inhaled deeply as she stepped in the door. The scents of various teas blended together like a perfume. Displays of tea services and china cups decorated the room.

"Maybe I'll get some green tea," Stella announced, examining the different blends for sale. "I drink it all the time. It's very good for you, full of antioxidants that prevent aging."

"They must work," Becky commented. "You certainly don't look as if you've aged."

Stella turned a grateful look on her friend. "Do you mean it?"

"I wouldn't have said it if I didn't mean it."

"It's true, Stella," Patty added. "You look great."

Before anyone could comment further, Wilhelm moved forward to introduce himself. "Welcome to Time for Tea. Jane, who are these lovely ladies?"

Jane introduced her friends, and Wilhelm turned on his considerable charm. "I've got hot water in the back. Would you like to sample some teas?" The women nodded, and Wilhelm began to set out dainty cups and saucers on the counter.

• • •

"You should have brought us here right away," Stella said to Jane over a steaming cup of oolong. "I have to buy some of this to take home."

"I want this." Becky held up a teapot that looked like a yellow duck with a spout for a beak and a handle in its tail feathers.

As Jane watched the shopping frenzy in progress, she leaned across the counter to Wilhelm. "I think it's your charm that's sold them."

Wilhelm chuckled as he wrapped the packages the others had purchased.

"Thank you, Jane," Wilhelm said. "I haven't had this many sales in a single hour in a long time."

"Glad to help. I hope business improves."

"Fortunately, my mail-order business for my china has picked up considerably lately. I've been busy searching for replacement cups, saucers and plates for some of my customers. It takes a good deal of time, communicating with other dealers."

"I hear you're going to be doing some traveling too. South America, isn't it?" Jane recalled Alice telling her about Florence's comment in the Coffee Shop earlier.

Much to Jane's astonishment, Wilhelm's eyes widened and he looked surreptitiously from right to left, as though he were afraid someone might have heard her comment.

"How do you know that?"

"Alice heard it in town."

Suddenly Wilhelm looked very worried. "In town?"

"What's the problem? You travel all the time."

"That is the price you pay for living in a little place like this. People think they know your business better than you do."

"I'm sorry. I can see you're upset." Jane glanced over her shoulder. Her friends were busy admiring a wicker table and chair in the window, set with items for a formal tea.

"I *am* planning to go to South America," Wilhelm said quietly, "but nothing is finalized yet. I haven't shared the news with my mother." Wilhelm and his elderly mother lived together and he was very solicitous of her. "Mother is more nervous about my traveling than she used to be. Too much twenty-four-hour-a-day television news, I think. She's especially down on South America right now. She's been reading about drug cartels and who knows what else in news magazines. Her worries are unfounded, of course. I'm a very cautious and experienced traveler. Still, I don't want her to know I'm going yet. I want to break the news to her gently."

Wilhelm looked pleadingly at Jane. "You do understand, don't you? If Mother were to hear this from someone else, it would upset her terribly. I can't understand how it even got out. Only a few people know about my plans."

Not anymore, Jane thought to herself. *Plenty of*

people already know if Ethel and Florence were privy to the information.

"I'm sorry you're worried. Maybe you should speak with your mother soon—just in case." Jane grimaced. "And I'll try to squelch the rumor in town," she added.

I'll speak to Aunt Ethel, she thought. *This is one time seemingly harmless gossip could actually cause some trouble.* Wilhelm's elderly mother was fragile. The last thing she needed was to worry more about her son's safety.

By the time Jane and the others got home late Thursday afternoon, Alice and Mary had Mary's quilt blocks completed and Claire was helping them to lay out the pieces on the floor in the sunroom in an appealing pattern.

"Next time I'm going to make something larger. This will be great as a wall hanging, but now I want to make some-thing bed-sized," Mary said as she surveyed her creation proudly.

"You put us to shame," Stella said, obviously delighted with how popular her idea to make quilts had been.

"Claire, you're almost done too," Sylvia said. "Shall I help you finish it up? Let's take it into the sunroom."

"I'm going to lie down for a few minutes," Patty said with a yawn and mounted the stairs to her room. Becky trailed into the sunroom to help Claire.

That left Jane and Stella alone in the dining room.

"Jane, does Patty seem . . . different . . . to you?" Stella asked. "She's much quieter than she used to be, don't you think?"

"Maybe she's got something on her mind."

"Surely she could tell us what it was. We are her best friends, after all." Stella hesitated. "Or at least we *were*. I'd like us to be close again—like old times."

Jane watched Stella, sure that Stella had never known the extent of Patty's resentment or jealousy. And now she didn't know about the guilt Patty carried either.

" 'O, what a tangled web we weave, When first we practice to deceive . . .' " Jane murmured to herself, remembering the words of Sir Walter Scott that her father often quoted.

Stella pulled out a chair and sat down. "I remember how beautiful I always thought Patty was when we were in school. Here I was, dark-haired and angular and she, so blonde, curvy and lovely. I hate to admit it, but I was jealous of her." Jane tried not to let the astonishment show on her face.

Stella stared out the window at a bird perched on a feeder. "Why do you think I try so hard at everything, Jane? My husband says it's because I'm afraid of not measuring up."

"If that's the case, none of us had any idea. You're a great actress."

Stella looked at Jane with fondness. "But being

with you guys for even a few hours makes me feel—real. It's not much fun pretending all the time. It doesn't seem so important to have to measure up here." Stella stood and wrapped her arms around Jane. "You are a good friend. Thank you for listening." She pulled back and flushed, as if embarrassed to have shared so much. "I think it's time for me to start sewing again."

Late in the afternoon Claire found Louise in the kitchen enjoying a cup of tea.

"Could we talk a little?" The young woman asked nervously. "I have something to tell you."

"Of course." Louise placed her cup down on the table and gestured to the empty chair.

"I've come to realize that I acted like a spoiled brat," Claire said. She took a deep breath. "It's time I grew up and apologized to my husband. I'm going to call him. I'm ready to go home."

Chapter Thirteen

D inner is served."
"It's about time," Becky said. "We're dying in here. It's cruel and unusual punishment to keep us away from the food, Jane."

"Whatever you're serving, it smells divine," Stella declared.

Stella, Patty and Becky were playfully pouting about being told to stay in the sunroom and out of the dining room for a half hour before dinner. Mary and Claire were more content, having started to work a jigsaw puzzle.

"I'm glad you stayed for dinner," Becky said to Claire as she put a hand on her shoulder. "Louise said you were going home."

"I'd planned to, but I called Ben's office and they told me he'd left for the day. I called home, but he wasn't there. Wouldn't you know it? Now, when I *want* to talk to him, I can't reach him. I'd rather stay here than rattle around in my empty house if he's gone somewhere. I had to insist that I start paying for my meals, however. I don't want to take advantage of the Howards' generosity."

"I know exactly what you mean," Mary said. "I wish I had a place to go so I wouldn't impose on them so much."

"You will soon," Claire said. "You are making progress."

Mary nodded but didn't look convinced. Instead, she picked up a puzzle piece and slid it into place.

It was later than their usual mealtime, and dusk was falling when Jane finally ushered them all into the dining room. The room was elegant, illuminated by candlelight, the table replete with linen and lace, mirrored tiles, flowers, crystal and lovely old china.

There was a breathless silence as the guests entered the glittering room.

"It's beautiful!" Stella finally exclaimed.

Louise, who was standing in the kitchen door with Jane and Alice, chuckled. "Jane's fixed something special for dinner. Alice got busy on the computer and made menus for you at each setting," Louise said.

"Take your places, please." Alice fluttered around the room. "Dinner is ready."

Patty sat down and picked up her personal menu.

Cold Cream of Cucumber Soup
Baby Greens with Cranberries
Dilled Salmon with Sour Cream Sauce
Wild and White Rice with Mushrooms
Brussels Sprouts with Pistachios
Chocolate Truffle & Toffee Cheesecake

"I've eaten in a lot of lovely places, but this is my favorite," Patty declared.

They'd all taken their places at the table, and Jane was about to serve the cold soup from a tureen on the sideboard when the doorbell rang.

"Who could that be?" Louise wondered aloud as she moved to get the door.

The others waited silently, and soon they could hear a male voice in the hall. The muted conversation went on for some moments. Then Louise reentered the room. She was followed by a tall, well-built man, handsome, with high cheekbones, a shock of thick brown hair and wide, hazel eyes.

"Claire, you have a visitor," Louise said.

Claire jumped to her feet. Pure delight lit her face. "Ben!" She ran to him, then threw herself into his arms. "What are you doing here?"

The man, eyeing the other women around the table, cleared his throat, obviously trying to decide if this was the time and place to say what he had to say.

He glanced again at Claire and made up his mind.

"I came to get you," the man said. "We need to talk."

"How did you find me?"

"I called the credit card company and found out where you'd been charging things. You purchased gas at the filling station in Acorn Hill so I drove over here to look for you. I saw your car parked here when I drove into town."

"You did all that to find me?"

"Of course I did. I love you, Claire." Ben's voice softened and he took her hands in his. "Please come home with me. I know I made you angry, but I'll make it up to you. I promise."

"There's nothing to make up for," she said, shaking her head. "I behaved like a spoiled child." She sighed. "Next year, if I want a birthday card, I'll write the date on your calendar in red letters."

Ben cleared his throat. "About that . . ."

Jane started to wonder if the rest of the group

should leave the room, though everyone at the table was thoroughly enjoying the love story unfolding before their eyes.

"Yes?"

"I didn't forget your birthday, exactly. I remembered, but was off on the date. You have to come home. You're having a surprise party tomorrow night at our house."

"I am?"

"I invited people weeks ago," Ben said sheepishly. "I just planned the party for the wrong week."

A look of astonishment and then chagrin flickered on Claire's features. "You planned a party for me?"

"People are coming from all over. What would they have said if they'd arrived and you were nowhere to be found?" Ben put his finger into the tight ring of his shirt collar.

Claire turned to Louise. "It seems I'll be checking out tonight."

"I should say so!" Louise said delightedly.

After Claire ran upstairs to get her things, Ben apologized for interrupting the ladies' dinner.

Jane insisted that he sit down at Claire's place to wait for her.

Soon Claire returned with her suitcase. Her eyes shone. In one hand she carried the lap quilt she and Louise had been working on.

Claire stopped in front of Louise. "You have

been so wonderful to me that I . . ." she choked up.

Louise reached out and took the fabric from her hand. "Why don't you leave this with me. I'll put the binding on it and send it to you."

"You don't have to do that."

"I *want* to do it. We don't want you to forget your visit to Grace Chapel Inn and the new beginning that happened here, do we?"

"Oh, believe me, I'm never going to forget that." Impulsively she kissed Louise on the cheek.

"Jane, I guess you'll get your bed back tonight," Mary joked.

Ben got to his feet, and he and Claire began walking toward the door. Then he turned back. "By the way, ladies, we're having a big party at our house tomorrow night if any of you want to come."

The couple departed to gales of laughter.

"Louise, you're a marriage counselor," Alice said.

"Well, I'm not sure what just happened," Mary ventured, "but it was wonderful."

"Now can we eat?" Becky pleaded.

Jane went back to ladling the soup into bowls. "It's a good thing I'd planned a *cold* soup tonight."

The phone rang just as they were all finishing dinner. Louise went to answer it.

"Louise? It's Carlene Moss. I heard about your new guest." Carlene was the editor of the *Acorn Nutshell* and a dedicated journalist. "What a great story! Amnesia! I wanted to see if it would be okay for me to stop at the inn and interview her."

"Can you hold for a moment, Carlene?" Louise asked. "I'll speak to Mary." Louise laid the phone on the desk and hurried back to the dining room.

"Mary, may Carlene Moss, the editor of our local newspaper, take your picture for the next issue? She wants to do a story on you." She glanced at the clock. "I can put her off if you aren't up to it tonight."

"An article? I'd like that very much. I want my face out there where people can see it." Mary ran her fingers through her hair. "If she wants to do it tonight, I'd better find a comb first." She got up from the table and headed for the stairs.

Louise went back to the telephone. "It's fine with Mary for you to come now."

"Wonderful," Carlene said breathlessly. "I'll be there soon."

It wasn't even five minutes later when they heard Carlene's car tires crunching on the driveway outside. Jane was carrying the truffle cheesecake into the dining room with a flourish. Her friends always insisted that chocolate was a major food group, so she knew this particular recipe was going to be a hit. They heard Carlene's car door slam, and moments later she rang the bell. Alice got up to let her in. A heated debate over the merits of dark versus milk chocolate, and the value of store-bought pie crust, was raging when they returned.

After introducing her friends to Carlene, Jane explained the conversation she had interrupted. "We eat food, we cook food and we talk about food. Food has been at least sixty percent of the entertainment since my friends have been here."

"We will also take a reminder of Jane's food home with us," Becky said, patting her midsection. "And have to buy bigger clothing because of it."

"You look very businesslike," Louise said, taking in the camera bag and Carlene's ever-present notebook. Carlene's brown hair was pulled back into a short ponytail, and her reading glasses were perched on the top of her head. She was dressed in a khaki pants suit with a white shirt.

"I'm on my way home from Potterston. A young woman from there is part of a group traveling to Tanzania as part of a mission trip. I wanted to get a photo of the group getting on the bus to the airport."

"How wonderful," Louise said, ushering her toward an empty chair. "I enjoy hearing about young people making a difference in the world."

"She was quite excited, as was the rest of the group. The experience will be life-changing for them, I'm sure."

Carlene hiked her camera bag higher onto her shoulder. "And of course I heard about the amnesia story and knew I had to get that into the next issue."

"We're very eager to get Mary's story out," Alice

said. "Maybe someone will come forward with information."

"It's a good idea. Many times eyewitnesses have no idea they've seen something out of the ordinary until they hear about an incident later." Carlene nodded approvingly.

At that moment, Mary walked down the stairs from the second floor. She was carrying Wendell, who was purring like a small motor. Mary settled Wendell on the floor. He made a figure eight through her legs before wandering off.

"This is Carlene Moss of the *Acorn Nutshell*," Louise said to Mary. "She's the one who has come to take a few pictures of you for the paper."

"That's wonderful. Maybe someone will recognize me." She turned to Carlene. "If you have any questions for me, I'd be happy to answer them."

Louise smiled. Asking Carlene if she had any questions was like asking Fred Humbert if he had any hardware. Newspaperwoman that she was, Carlene loved asking questions. "You can use the sunroom. The rest of us will be dallying over dessert for a while, no doubt. I'll bring you some while you visit."

Ethel arrived just in time to get the last piece of cheesecake.

"How is your project working out?" Jane inquired, referring to her budding friendship with LeAnn.

"Frankly, I think Florence is overdoing it a little, being neighborly, I mean. She's going to suffocate the poor woman with sisterly love. If I want to visit with her, I practically have to go to the post office and stand at the counter to do so."

"It sounds as though you and Florence are in competition for LeAnn's attention," Jane observed mildly. Ethel didn't seem to notice.

"The post office is an interesting place, however," Ethel continued. "I've caught up with people I haven't seen in months . . . like that poor Billings couple. *Tsk. Tsk. Tsk.* I really do love the people in this community and hate it when any of them are having troubles."

"I told Alice and Jane that I would talk to Mr. and Mrs. Billings the next time I saw them," Louise said. "Perhaps they'll confide in me. If so, I'd be happy to help them with their bookkeeping."

"You are such a dear person, Louise," Ethel said. "I only wish we could solve everyone's problems so easily."

Mary and Carlene came back into the dining room, interview finished. Carlene said her goodbyes and left. Mary sat down wearily and motioned for them to continue their conversation.

"There are other troubles?" Jane asked, looking at Ethel questioningly.

Ethel nodded. "Like Jean Humbert not telling her mother she has a boyfriend in Australia."

"But Aunt Ethel, are you sure that's *true*?" Alice asked.

"Aunt Ethel, I know for a fact it *isn't* true," Louise said. "I was visiting with Vera and Jean today at the hardware store. Jean is working there this summer. Viola came in, and while we all were chatting she asked Jean if she had a boyfriend in Australia. Vera and Jean thought it was the funniest thing they'd ever heard. Apparently Jean has a steady boyfriend at college. Vera said she wouldn't be surprised if they considered marriage someday. Besides, Jean and Vera are very close. Jean would never keep something like that from her mother."

"No boyfriend in Australia? How can that be?" Ethel got an odd look on her face. "But my source is so dependable."

"It is lovely to hear of a mother and daughter that close," Mary said, unaware of Ethel's sudden turmoil or what the Howard sisters might be thinking of this new bit of information. "I wonder if *I* have children."

"You're sad because you don't even know if you are a mother, and ever since I arrived, I've been wondering why I had children in the first place. What an ungrateful person I am," Becky said.

Mary looked bewildered.

"Perhaps I need to explain," Becky said, recognizing the confusion the statement had caused around the room. Her gaze fell on Stella and Patty. "We've been having trouble with Blaine. He recently dropped out of school, quit his job, lost his apartment and came home to live with us. He's been living in his old room in our basement ever since. He watches television all day and shows no inclination or ambition whatsoever to look for a job."

"That's not the Blaine we've always heard about," Patty said.

"He goes out at night after we've gone to bed and comes home in the wee hours of the morning. His father and I have talked until we're blue in the face, but it doesn't faze him. It's as if he doesn't even hear us."

Becky reached for a tissue in her pocket. "His father is furious. He says that we've raised a 'lazy, good-for-nothing.' You know how much I dislike conflict. I'd go to any lengths to avoid it but now I'm living with it every day." She dabbed at her eyes. "I've been miserable."

"Just because your adult son is making decisions you don't like doesn't mean you have to blame yourself for it," Stella said. "You've been a great mom, but you can't mother your children forever. They need to try their own wings."

"I'm not sure he has wings," Becky said miserably. "I thought I was such a good mother. I taught my children morals and values. They know Jesus. They went to church, to piano lessons, to soccer and volleyball. We scrimped and saved to put them through wonderful schools and now . . . I thought I knew my children, but apparently I was wrong. What's worse—and completely selfish—is that I think it's a reflection on my parenting."

"Has he seen a doctor or a counselor?" asked Alice. "It could be that he is depressed."

"What would he have to be depressed about?"

"It's not always as simple as that," Alice said quietly.

"My husband says—"

"What do you say, Becky?" Patty asked.

Becky looked around the room silently, watching the faces of her friends. Then she stood up. "If you'll excuse me, I want to call home," she said just audibly. "I let my ego stand in the way of helping my son. If my son is in trouble and not just lazy as my husband believes, then . . . well . . . I'm not sure quite what I'll do yet, but I'll think of something."

"We're a messed-up bunch, aren't we?" Stella mused as she, Jane and Patty sat on the darkened front porch later that evening. A bull-frog chorus rumbled in the distance. "I had no idea this trip would have such an effect on all of us."

"What's happened for you, Stella?" Patty asked softly.

Stella poured herself more iced tea from a carafe on the table. "I've realized how much I've missed my old friends. The people I know in the art world are acquaintances, but most of them aren't true friends. Right now I'm fairly 'hot.' I can't tell who actually wants to be my friend and who just wants to say they hang out with Stella Leftner."

"That's sad," Patty said, shaking her head.

"My husband says that old friends are the best. Despite all the people he knows, who does Al go hiking and watch baseball with? The guys he knew in high school and two college roommates. They have stood the test of time and he trusts them."

Stella's gaze was steady as she studied her friends. "Like you all," Stella murmured. "I can trust you."

"I had no idea you cared so much," Patty said.

"I've always admired you, Patty. We had our differences, but you were my role model, whether you knew it or not. I've always been impulsive, hurrying to finish something so I could go on to something else. You, on the other hand, are meticulous. You taught me how to pace myself and really evaluate what I was doing, especially in my art. I've thanked you silently many times over the years for your example." Stella smiled. "Even if you seemed just too good to be true sometimes."

"But I was jealous of you," Patty said, her voice barely a whisper.

"I would have given my pinkie finger just to look like you back then. I even considered coloring my hair blonde." Stella touched her dark hair. "We always fell for the same men and I was sure I was going to lose every one of them to you."

"I thought it was the other way around!" Patty marveled. "You were tiny, thin and exotic. You reminded me of a hummingbird, touching down at every flower. I could never keep up with you. If I'd been a bird, I would have had to have been . . . an ostrich."

"It would have made things easier if we'd known all this back then, wouldn't it?" Stella concluded cheerfully. "We certainly wasted a lot of time and energy wishing to be some-thing we're not," Stella put her slender hand over Patty's. "I'm glad that I got to say these things to you. Now that we are older and wiser, we can finally put that undercurrent of competition between us to rest."

Before Patty or Jane could speak, Stella continued, "Speaking of maturing, I'd like to run something by you, ladies. I'm thinking of having a face-lift."

"You can't have one of those unless you actually have something to lift." Jane pointed out.

"My jawline is looking a little soft, don't you think?" Stella cranked her head to the right and to the left. "There are some significant crow's-feet here." She pointed to her eyes.

"You need new glasses, not a face-lift," Patty said.

"You wouldn't tell me a big fib just to make me feel better, would you?" Stella looked cheered.

"We've quit comparing ourselves to others," Patty said, "remember?"

Stella turned to Jane. "How about you?"

"Honestly? Real friend to real friend?"

"Of course."

"This reminds me of a verse in Samuel," Jane said. " 'The Lord does not look at the things man looks at. Man looks at the outward appearance, but the Lord looks at the heart' (1 Samuel 16:7)." Jane put her hand over her heart. "It's in *here* that people need a lift and there is only one Physician competent to do that."

"A spirit lift, huh?" Stella smiled. "You always did know how to put things in perspective."

They sat in companionable silence, each buried in her own thoughts until Stella glanced at her watch. "Ugh. I have to call the gallery tonight. Someone has questions for me about a piece of my work. If you'll excuse me, I'll take care of that now."

When she was gone, Patty turned to Jane. "Stella is offering me the friendship that I've longed for with her," she said quietly. "What if my deception spoils it all?"

"You were young," Jane said. "You've already paid a high price for what you did. It's time to come clean, Patty. Tell Stella. You heard what she said about true friends. Trust her to be one of yours."

"I know, I know," Patty sighed. "But it's too late tonight. Now it will have to wait until morning."

Chapter Fourteen

Jane found Alice at the computer early on Friday morning and paused to peer over her sister's shoulder.

"I couldn't sleep, so I'm doing research on missing persons," Alice informed her. "I'm trying to find something that will tell me about people who have been reported missing in Pennsylvania in the past week. Then I plan to look at all the states that border us. Surely if Mary wandered off, someone has reported her missing by now."

"Don't you think the police have already done that kind of search?"

Alice sighed and her hands dropped limply into her lap. "I suppose so, but I feel like I need to do *something*."

"Thanks to you she has a roof over her head, food to eat and clothing to wear, and soon," Jane said with a smile, "her very own lap quilt. She's safe, and we're praying for her. Don't sell yourself short, Alice."

"A social worker from the hospital said that as long as Mary was with us, she felt Mary was in good hands. But . . ."

"I understand. I've been thinking about it too. We can't keep her forever. Nor would she want us to."

Jane looked at the site Alice had put on the screen. "Maybe there's another way."

"There hasn't been any news coverage yet. The *Acorn Nutshell* article will be out next week, but maybe we can get more newspapers interested in her story." Alice spoke with determination. "What we need is to draw attention to her situation."

"And how do you propose we go about that?"

At that moment Stella drifted into the room in workout clothes. "Go about what?"

"Good morning. Where are you going so early?" Jane asked.

"Jogging. I talked Patty and Becky into going with me. That should be interesting since neither of them has run in years. Would you like to come?" Stella peered curiously over Alice's shoulder just as Jane had.

"No thanks. I have a few things to take care of." Jane often enjoyed jogging in the morning, but she had her hands full making breakfast for the large group today.

"What were you talking about when I came in? 'Go about' what?"

"Alice is on the Internet trying to find out about persons reported missing in the last few days. She thinks we should put more effort into finding out who Mary is."

"Media coverage," Stella said nonchalantly. "When I'm opening a new show or my husband has something big at his gallery, we always try to get an interview with someone—a feature article or a radio interview on a morning show, for example.

It's amazing how many people tune in while they drink their coffee and read the paper. Al does a casual tracking of where people have heard about the gallery events, and a number always say they heard it on the radio."

Alice nodded sagely. "Exactly. No one can come forward and identify her if they don't even know what's happened."

"Acorn Hill isn't really media central of the universe. How does one go about attracting attention?" Jane asked.

"You've got to have a hook," Stella said confidently. "An angle."

"Isn't a woman who doesn't know who she is angle enough?" Alice asked.

"Perhaps we're thinking on too large a scale," Jane said. "We need to start smaller. I'm sure there are lots of people right here in Acorn Hill who haven't heard about Mary."

"That's true," Stella acquiesced. "And she was found not far from town. Maybe someone saw or heard something and he or she doesn't even realize it. I'll talk about this with Becky and Patty on our run. When we get back, we'll do some brainstorming. See you in forty-five minutes." She headed for the front porch where her friends were waiting.

Alice followed Jane into the kitchen where Jane put on water for tea and brewed a pot of coffee.

"What could we do that would make a difference?" Jane asked. "We need to do something to keep Mary's hopes up."

Alice, meanwhile, stared at the kettle as if she were willing it to boil. The moment it started whistling, she rose and poured the water into the teapot.

"What *do* you think happened to her, Alice?"

Alice brought the teapot and cups to the table and sat down. "I've thought about it a lot. The first thing we have to account for is the way Mary was battered and bruised when she was found."

"There aren't too many ways to explain that, are there?"

"It would be easy if she'd been in a car accident. That would explain everything. The problem is that there was no car."

"And therefore, no accident."

"That's what makes it so suspicious. If it didn't happen in an accident, she must have been responsible for her condition . . . or someone else caused it."

The sisters were quiet as they contemplated the possibilities. Finally Jane stood up and walked to the refrigerator. She took out eggs and milk, then began to mix together some waffle batter.

A short while later, there was a commotion in the front hall as Stella and the others returned.

"We're starving!" Patty called into the kitchen. "Stella worked us like a fiend."

"I've never been so exhausted." Becky came into

the kitchen and draped herself over a chair. "I may need chocolate to revive me."

"Hah! They walked and complained the entire way," said Stella.

"Here, have some fruit." Jane pushed a serving dish heaped with fresh fruit toward Becky. Becky frowned.

"I'm working on waffles."

"That sounds more like it," Becky said, dimpling sweetly as she smiled at Jane. "They're at least as good for me as a run, don't you think? Replacing carbs and all that?"

"See my problem?" Stella continued. "They don't take me seriously. Becky looked around, commenting on the birds, flora and fauna and how she needed to get out and sketch. Patty kept saying she was out of breath. The only reason she was out of breath was because she was talking so much."

"The woman is a general," Patty insisted, "barking orders, yelling at us to keep up."

"Sounds like not much has changed in twenty-plus years," Jane said. She poured some batter on the sizzling waffle iron.

Soon everyone was seated around the kitchen table. Mary came down and offered to pour coffee.

"Delish!" Stella took a bite of waffle and closed her eyes. "This is my new favorite food."

"Apparently a little fresh air did you all good," Louise observed as she entered the room.

Jane turned to Stella. "Maybe you'd better not

take them running again. It seems to perk up their appetites. I may not have enough food in the house to feed them."

"It's your own fault," Stella retorted cheerfully. "You are too fine a cook, that's all."

Mary took a seat at the table. "I was thinking about jogging. I should try it, I guess. My body will tell me if it is something I've done before or not."

"You should do that," Jane said. "If you like it, great. If not, that's okay too."

Alice cleared her throat. "We were discussing your situation this morning, Mary. We'd like to think of a way to let more people know about your plight. It occurred to us that someone right here in Acorn Hill might know something."

"The police have sent my photo to a number of places, but they've had no response. It's as if I didn't exist at all. How could it be that someone here would recognize me?"

"Someone may have noticed a strange car going through town or driving down the road where you were found. Who knows?"

Jane snapped her fingers. "I've got an idea. You've mentioned how grateful you are that Finn found you. Why don't we have a little garden party and invite Finn and Kieran? I know Kieran would appreciate it. I've heard around town that he's telling people how proud he is of his 'rescue' dog. We'll just let it be known that it is an open house to honor Finn and that we're hoping that someone might have seen something and will come forward. We'd be grateful for anyone who might be able to help in any way."

"Won't that be a lot of work?"

"Jane could prepare for it with one arm tied behind her back," Alice said confidently.

"We talked only a week or so ago about having something here just to show off the flowers. I think this is a wonderful idea. Two birds with one stone, so to speak," Louise said.

"We'll call it a reception for you and Finn," Jane said. "You can never tell who might have information he doesn't even know he—or she—has. And the media might see this as a good hook," she said, smiling at Stella. "Besides, it will be fun. You all can get a feel for the people of Acorn Hill."

"The weather is supposed to be perfect on Sunday," Alice said. "Can we be ready by then?"

"Certainly. We'll make cookies and have Clarissa bake a cake at the Good Apple. We can use flowers from the garden for the table."

"And I'll polish the silver tea service," Louise announced.

Alice bobbed her head. "We'll take the long tables we've been using for our sewing machines outside. I'll cover them with our lace cloths."

"Oh my," said a small voice. Mary's eyes were huge and she'd gone very pale. "All this for me?"

"Do you mind?" Alice asked. "We should have

asked your permission before we pushed ahead and started making plans."

"Mind? When you want to do something so wonderful for me?" Mary gave them a warm, thankful smile. "Perhaps someone will know who I am. And if they don't, at least we've tried. Besides, Finn *is* the real hero in this story. People should hear what an animal like Finn is capable of doing."

"So we can go ahead?" Stella asked, obviously itching to get started.

"Only if you'll tell me what I can do to help," Mary said.

"We can help Jane bake cookies," Becky suggested.

"If I remember correctly you always ate more than you baked," Patty commented.

"Okay, we can help with the baking," Stella said, "But there must be more that we can do. How about weeding the flowerbeds?"

"I like that idea," Jane teased. "Becky, can I borrow your camera? We'll need to have proof that you three ever picked weeds."

"Not to worry, girls. Weeds don't dare grow in Jane's garden," Alice said.

"That's a relief," Patty said. "I don't like weeding."

"We forgot one big item," Jane said. "Before we go much further we'd better see if Finn and his master can come."

"May I call him?" Mary asked shyly. "I'd like to be the one to invite them."

"Why don't you take the phone into the library," Alice suggested. "It's too noisy here. We'll get busy as soon as he gives us an answer."

Just after Mary went off to the library, the front door opened and Sylvia called, "Anybody home?"

"In the kitchen," Jane answered her.

"What's going on in here?" Sylvia asked when she entered the kitchen. "It smells divine."

"Pecan waffles. Want one?"

Sylvia went to the cupboard and got a plate. "Is there coffee?"

"I just finished brewing a new pot."

Again, Sylvia went to the cupboard for a mug and poured a cup of coffee for herself.

"Thanks for making yourself at home here," Jane said. "Some days I need as many hands as an octopus has tentacles to get things done."

"Treat friends like family and family like friends," Sylvia said.

"I'd like to add to that," Stella said. "At Grace Chapel Inn they just treat everyone like royalty."

"Trust me," Jane replied, "we wouldn't serve royalty in our kitchen."

"What are you doing here so early in the morning?" Louise asked Sylvia.

"I lay in bed last night thinking about the quilts. I decided, if you'd let me, that I'd machine-quilt the tops for you. Because they're lap-sized, it won't take me more than an hour or two."

Sylvia sat down. "Then you'll each have your

own special memory of Grace Chapel Inn to take home with you."

"How nice of you," Jane said, pouring some batter onto the hot waffle iron for a fresh waffle.

"Mine's a prayer quilt," Becky murmured. "As I sewed, I prayed for Blaine and the wisdom to know how to help him."

The room grew quiet as they considered her statement.

"I tried to call Blaine last night. He didn't pick up the phone, but I knew he was there. He's always home. Maybe he looked at caller ID, saw it was me and decided he didn't want to talk."

"He wouldn't do that to you." Patty hesitated. "Would he?"

"Frankly? I don't know what he'd do anymore. He's put a wall around himself. Nothing gets in and nothing gets out. I was tempted to give him a piece of my mind when the answering machine came on, but I decided against it. Instead, I told him that whatever else happened, I will always love him. He's my son no matter what he does with his life." Becky gave a small, humorless laugh.

"I'm sure what he needs most is unqualified acceptance," Stella said. "It's what we've all longed for at one time or another."

"I've been so upset with him that I've neglected to tell him how much I love him. I've never recognized until now how much of myself I've tied up in my children," Becky admitted. "Somehow I've got to learn to let go." Everyone was suddenly silent as Patty gave Becky a warm hug.

Jane saw that emotions were near the surface and deliberately changed the subject. She put a stack of cookbooks on the table. "Here is some reading material, ladies. There are decisions to be made. What kinds of sweets shall we serve at our party?"

Louise quickly explained to Sylvia about the party, and everyone started talking at once and moved closer to the table. Jane then added to the stack one of the files that held her tried-and-true cookie and candy recipes. "You might also want to look in here. And let's think of a gift to present to Kieran as a small token of appreciation."

Chapter Fifteen

Viola Reed was behind the counter when Jane entered Nine Lives Bookstore. She'd left her friends in charge of picking out some recipes for the party, and she and Sylvia had walked to town, laden with lap quilts. Jane dropped off Sylvia at her store, then continued on to the bookstore to look for a gift for Kieran.

"Hello, stranger, I haven't seen you for a few days." Viola's face lit up at the sight of Jane.

"Hi, Viola. My college roommates are here for a reunion, so we've been busy at the inn. You may actually have heard of one of them." Jane mentioned Becky's name, and Viola's eyes grew wide.

"The illustrator?" Viola brought her hand to her throat and reflexively rearranged the rainbow colored scarf tied artfully at her neck. "I have some of the books she's illustrated here in the store. They're very popular." She walked to the children's section and pulled a couple of Becky's books from the shelf. "You don't think she would . . ."

"Stop by and autograph them for you?"

"Yes." Viola clasped her hands together.

"I'll ask her. I'm sure she will if she has time. Or you can bring them to her. We've got a lot on our plates these days. That's why I came to talk to you." Jane gave Viola the Cliffs Notes version of what they were planning.

". . . and I wondered if you could recommend a book that Kieran Morgan might enjoy. My friends and I thought that a book would be an appropriate gift. Nothing elaborate, just something to present to him as a token of appreciation."

"He comes in here every once in a while and looks at books on Ireland. I have a lovely picture book of the countryside. I also have CDs of Irish music." Viola looked a little embarrassed. "I like that kind of music. It makes me want to kick up my heels."

Jane tried to picture the thickset woman doing a sprightly jig, but couldn't quite imagine it.

"If you are free on Sunday afternoon, we'd love to have you join us," Jane said as Viola gift-wrapped the book.

"Why, I'd be delighted to come."

"The party will be from two until five. Drop in anytime. Please let your customers know about it. We're counting on word of mouth." She started toward the door.

"I'll be happy to pass on the invitation. *Er*, Jane, before you go . . ." Viola hesitated. "Your Aunt Ethel was in here this morning saying the most peculiar things."

Jane turned back to Viola. "What kinds of things?"

"That she was afraid that Clarissa Cottrell might retire and move away from Acorn Hill. And something about an old couple who are in financial trouble. I didn't quite catch who they were. Surely *I* would have heard if any of that were true. I'm in the store every day and people, well, talk. But if there's anything we can do to help that poor couple, we should. Could you find out from your aunt who they are so we can see what kind of help they need?"

Jane had a suspicion she knew where Ethel's information came from. "I'll talk to her about it," Jane said, then smiled at Viola and walked out the door. Book tucked under her arm, Jane walked slowly back towards Sylvia's Buttons, her mind in a whirl. She should head to the inn, but she needed Sylvia's advice.

"While you ladies are looking at recipes, I think I'll go on an errand of my own," Louise announced soon after Jane and Sylvia had left. "On the way home I'll stop at the store for some eggs and butter. I imagine we'll be needing more."

She took a jar of homemade preserves from the cupboard and went upstairs for her purse. Louise had decided that now was as good a time as any to check on Nanette and Oscar Billings.

The elderly couple lived on the other side of Acorn Hill, but Louise decided to walk. She needed time to formulate what she might say to let this couple know that if they needed help in straightening out their financial affairs, she was available. She had to do it in such a way that would not insult them or have them think she was prying.

Lord, I pray for wisdom, tact and compassion. And for Your words on my lips.

Nanette and Oscar lived in a small green bungalow on a narrow lot in an older part of Acorn Hill. Louise remembered visiting the home with her father when she was a youngster. The Billingses must have been newlyweds at the time.

She lifted a hand to knock on the front door, but it opened before she could lower her knuckles. Oscar peered out at her like a friendly mole, blinking against the bright sun.

"Miss Louise, is that you?"

He'd always called the Howard sisters Miss Louise, Miss Alice and Miss Jane, a courtly gesture shown to three little girls.

"Hello, Oscar. I've been thinking of you lately and decided to pay you and Nanette a visit. I brought you a jar of Jane's preserves."

"Anything Miss Jane makes has to be delicious." He stepped aside. "Come in, come in. Nanette and I were in the kitchen, reading the papers."

The house's interior was just as she had remembered it—full of built-in, walnut bookshelves in the living room. In the dining room there was a floor-to-ceiling china cabinet filled with antique dishes. Most were flow blue—white dishes with blue designs that seemed to bleed into the pieces themselves and created a blurred effect. The china dated back to the late 1800s and, if Nanette ever wanted to sell it, the set would bring quite a price.

"Well look who's here!" A wavery voice greeted Louise. "How lovely of you to stop by."

Louise put the preserves on the table and gave the old woman a hug. "How are you? It's been far too long since I've seen you and Oscar."

Nanette tapped her hearing aid. "Can't hear very well at church anymore. These things aren't worth the plastic they're made from. Instead, we watch a TV preacher every Sunday morning and turn up the volume full blast. It's not as good as the real thing, of course, but God's with us too, just like you folks at church."

"I'm sure He is." Louise felt warmth spreading through her. She'd nearly forgotten how dear and sweet these people were.

"Can I get you something? Tea, coffee . . . ?"

"No. I'm fine."

"Some fruit then? Will you eat a pear or a nectarine? We'll never finish them all before they go bad."

Louise looked to where Nanette was pointing. A large basket of fresh fruit sat on the counter.

"My daughter must think we don't eat our fruits and vegetables," Nanette cackled. "She sends us stuff like that all the time. Please, will you eat something?"

Louise agreed to a pear and watched as Nanette washed it, put it on a plate along with a small knife and brought it to her. The elderly woman had a spring in her step and a lightness to her carriage that belied her true age. And she didn't look the least bit worried about anything. Had Aunt Ethel been imagining things?

"I was just thinking about your father and mother the other day," Oscar said as he joined them. "What a fine couple they were . . ."

The three of them spent the next few minutes reminiscing. Then Louise told them about the garden party on Sunday and invited them to come.

"It would be lovely to be at a party there again," Nanette said wistfully. "Your mother was such a fine cook and she loved to entertain."

"We'll be there with bells on," Oscar said jovially.

"No bells, dear," Nanette rejoined. "They are havoc for my hearing aids."

Louise was silently praying for guidance and for the right words to bring up the true reason for her visit when Nanette reached for a small photo album that was lying on the counter.

"You'll have to see photos of my grandchildren and great-grandchildren. We've got quite a family. They're such a blessing to us—and so much help."

" 'Help'?" Louise echoed.

"We haven't had to worry about things for years. My grandsons come and paint the house. My daughter hires someone to do our windows. My son-in-law, an accountant, even does our taxes for us. We're retired in style, I'd say." Nanette sat back with a smile on her face.

"An accountant?" Louise stammered. "He does your taxes?"

"Has for years. He was an investment counselor for a while too. Thanks to him, we haven't had to worry about getting along financially in our golden years. Bless his heart."

If Oscar and Nanette have significant invest-ments and an accountant in the family, it's not likely that they would have tax problems, Louise thought. *How had Aunt Ethel come to that conclu-sion?*

"He's recently been hired as a taxpayer advocate for the IRS," Oscar said. "And he's been sending us information from his office ever since. I've begun to wonder what the people at the post office must think with this blizzard of mail from the IRS coming our way."

"Now dear, he's being good to us, you know that. The least we can do is bring it home and look at it before we throw it away." Nanette turned to Louise. "Could you eat an orange, dear? Or a kiwi?"

Sylvia was in the back room using her long-arm quilting machine when Jane arrived at the store. Sylvia looked up and smiled as Jane walked in.

"I'm almost done with your friends' lap quilts. All they will have left is to sew the bindings. These quick little quilts have turned out rather well, I think."

Sylvia clipped a few threads and pulled Stella's three-by-three creation off the long arm and held it up. The rich colors made for a striking quilt, and Sylvia ran her fingers over the fabric fondly. "What do you think?"

"Fabulous. You're a genius. That's why I came to talk to you. You have to help me figure out what to do." Jane told Sylvia of her conversation with Viola and her suspicions that Ethel might be behind some of the other rumors currently going around town.

Sylvia ran her fingers through her hair. " 'A little knowledge is a dangerous thing.' Ethel is probably gathering snippets of information and running with them. The rumors could be hurtful to the people involved."

"Do you think I should say something to her?" Jane asked.

Sylvia shrugged. "That's up to you. It might mean a lot to the individuals affected."

Jane sighed. "I think I'll stop by the carriage house and try to ask some tactful questions." They chatted for a few more minutes. Then Jane headed toward Ethel's house.

On her way, she met Rev. Thompson.

"Hello, Jane." He greeted her with a warm smile. "I haven't seen you out and about the past couple days."

"I'm having a minireunion at the inn for some college friends. We've been too busy talking to go out much."

As they chatted, an idea flashed into her mind. "Would you be willing to make a brief announcement for me at church on Sunday?" She told him about the garden party, Mary and Finn.

"I certainly will. Even if it's not strictly church-related, it is an act of kindness. We should all be supporting Mary in any way we can. How many people are you expecting?"

"I don't know. It doesn't matter, really, since we're having it outside and the time is flexible. All I have to make sure of is that we have enough tea, cold drinks and sweets."

"I know what kind of baker you are. The idea of

the food alone may bring more people than you've bargained for."

Jane laughed.

"I'll spread the word, Jane. Today I'm doing church visits out near Fairy Pond. If anyone saw something, it would likely be someone who lives out there."

After she left the pastor, Jane kept on toward the carriage house. A lump formed in her stomach as she neared. How does one go about suggesting to one's beloved aunt that she is manufacturing and spreading rumors?

Of course, Ethel would never spread something she didn't think was true, but that didn't change the situation.

Jane knocked on the door and heard her aunt call "Come in."

Florence was with Ethel. Jane's heart sank. This would not be a good time to converse with her aunt. "You look busy."

Ethel gestured at a pile of flannel and some scissors on the table. "We're making items for layettes at church. A mother somewhere in the world will have some new things for her new baby. It's very exciting, don't you think?" Ethel said.

"Aunt Ethel, have you been bored lately?" Jane inquired impulsively, not quite sure where she was going with her question.

Her aunt tittered nervously. "Now why would you ask that?"

"Just curious, that's all. You've been spending a lot of time with LeAnn from the post office."

"A nice girl," Florence chimed in. "Much more relaxed than our other postmistress."

"What do you mean?"

"She is so much more open than Alma. LeAnn *says* things."

"Out of the ordinary things." Ethel jumped into the conversation. "Like who gets letters from interesting places."

"And she doesn't act so self-important either. You know how Alma is, laying all the letters face down on the counter, guarding the mail like someone might want to peek at it."

"She didn't happen to mention that someone in town was getting letters from the IRS, did she?" Jane tried to act nonchalant.

"She hasn't said that outright," Florence said, "but I saw . . . well, never mind. It just goes to show that we don't know our neighbors as well as we think we do."

"It certainly does," Jane said wearily. How could she ask her next question delicately? "Might it be best to make sure your information is correct before spreading it around town?"

"Oh, but I saw this with my own eyes," Florence said, nodding.

"Surely you have important tasks at the inn, dear," Ethel said. "Is there anything I can do to help?"

Jane sighed and decided she might as well ask her aunt and Florence to do what they were best at. She explained about the garden party. "You could let people know about the party and that we're hoping someone will step forward with information about the time Mary was found."

"We'll get right on it." Ethel turned back to her project, and Jane knew she had been dismissed.

Jane stood outside on her aunt's porch for a moment and sent up a quick prayer. *Lord, they mean so well. May there be a lesson for us in all of this.*

Jane headed back to the inn feeling particularly frustrated and yet sympathetic toward the two women. They definitely needed a new hobby.

Chapter Sixteen

How does this look?" Becky held up the sign she was making. Flowers erupted out of every corner, and a big red dog was sniffing at the posies in the lower right hand corner. The words on the poster read:

Garden Party at Grace Chapel Inn
Sunday, 2-5 PM
Come meet Mary and Finn

"Very nice. It's not often that the bulletin board in the grocery store holds a piece of original art." Jane measured ingredients into a bowl for a batch of lemon bars.

"Okay. Then I'll make more signs like this one."

"You don't have to work that hard," Jane said. "I'm sure that Mayor Tynan's secretary Bella would color photocopy that one for us."

Becky winced. "I don't think so. I'll keep drawing while the rest of you bake."

"Don't you think we have enough, Jane? I've never seen so many cookies and bars in my life." Stella stood back to look at the tower of filled plastic containers and the trays covered with sugar cookies, ginger snaps and tiny squares of something made with coconut, chocolate and caramels.

"What doesn't get eaten will go into the freezer. I like to keep things on hand for guests. I often put a plate of cookies and a carafe of coffee on the sideboard in the dining room in the afternoon. It's a little extra welcoming touch."

"So we're doing slave labor for you, in other words." Patty put a dab of pink frosting on a small white cookie.

"Something like that."

"Does anyone recall the time we helped Becky bake for that guy she felt sorry for?"

"That was before I met my husband," Becky said primly. "Ancient history. I was a mere slip of a child back then."

"You weren't very mature, we'll give you that."

Becky glared at Stella which, of course, didn't stop Stella.

"Could I help it that he fell madly, head-over-heels in love with me? It was *cookies*, not gold I gave him."

"He didn't leave you alone after that until—"

"Never mind." Becky put her finger to her lips. "No one is interested in hearing this again—"

"Oh come on. For old times' sake," Jane said.

Becky groaned while Stella told the story to Alice and Louise.

"She wanted him to stop following her around. One day Becky looked out the window of the front door and saw him walking down the sidewalk. She didn't have time to hide, and he would have seen her if she'd run to the back of the house."

Becky blushed the red of the geraniums in her artwork. "The only thing I could think of—I dropped to the floor in front of the door and lay there. I knew he couldn't see me so I thought that if I just lay still, he'd give up and go away."

"But he didn't go away," Patty picked up the story. "He kept knocking and knocking and when he didn't get an answer, he tried to open the front door so he could call inside."

"And there was Becky, lying on the floor, hiding out," Stella said.

"He never followed me again," Becky said with a sigh. "Of course he never spoke to me again either. I can't believe the things we did when we were young."

"We all did them, Beck," Stella said casually. "At least we outgrew our childishness. Not everyone does."

Patty drew a sharp breath but said nothing.

"You're shaking like a leaf," Alice observed. She and Mary were in the waiting room of the doctor's office in Potterston on Friday afternoon, looking forward to getting the doctor's take on Mary's improvement.

"I'm so nervous. I don't know if it's a good thing that I'm having faint recollections, or if that will be all I ever get. I need to know how to live if I never get my memory back." Mary gripped Alice's hands in her own.

"Let's not move to the worst case scenario quite yet," Alice said calmly.

"You may go in now," the receptionist announced to Mary.

Mary clutched Alice's hand. "Come with me?"

Instead of being shown into an exam room, they were invited into a private office. Dr. Broadmoor stood up, shook hands with them and gestured for them to sit down.

"You look much better," he said, examining the fading bruises on Mary's arms. He asked her some questions and made a few notes in a file. "Traumatic amnesia is usually transient," he said, "but the length of its duration often depends on the degree of the injury one sustains. You obviously had head trauma, but you've recovered well from your physical injuries."

Mary nodded. "Thanks to the Howard sisters."

Dr. Broadmoor smiled. "I understand how they could be good medicine." He shifted in his chair. "I've talked to a number of other doctors, experts about amnesia. What they all advise, at least for the time being, is that we be patient."

"There's that word again," Mary muttered.

"What, if anything, have you recalled since I saw you last?"

Mary told him about the things that had resonated within her.

"But I can't bring the memories fully to the surface."

"Still, it's progress. Things may come back gradually or pop into your head all at once. For now, our hospital social worker has told me that she has some good news. She's found several housing options for you. There are apartments in Potterston that . . ."

Mary looked at Alice with panic in her blue eyes. "I know I can't stay at the inn forever, but perhaps there is a room somewhere in Acorn Hill?" she asked pleadingly. "I don't need much. Just a bed and . . ."

"The housing facilities are maintained by the state and very low cost. Considering your . . .

financial situation, the social worker feels it might be best if . . ."

"I'm sure we can find a temporary situation that Mary finds tolerable," Alice said quickly. "Grace Chapel has offered funds from their outreach program to help Mary."

"Are you sure? The facilities are carefully maintained."

Alice saw that Mary's eyes were wide with fear. "We'd like her to stay with us."

The doctor nodded. "That's your decision."

"In the meantime, what can I *do*?"

The doctor smiled. "Have patience."

"And pray," Alice added softly.

Chapter Seventeen

My husband must be the dearest man on the planet," Stella announced to no one in particular as they all sat in the kitchen, watching Jane make their evening meal. Louise and Alice were bustling around the room helping to get the meal set up, and the aroma of fresh baked goods hung deliciously in the air.

"I just called to tell him what was happening, and do you know what he said to me? He said 'Sweet-ums, you just stay as long as you want. It sounds like a wonderful cause, and the gallery is practically running itself.' His secretary is dealing with my mail. All I have to do when I get home is go back to my studio and start painting again."

" 'Sweet-ums,' " Becky echoed. "He calls you 'Sweet-ums'?"

"You didn't hear a word I said, did you?" Stella wagged a finger at Becky.

"Of course I did," said Becky, grinning broadly. "Al sounds awesome. But 'Sweet-ums'? Now really . . ."

Stella picked a carrot off a plate of crudités on the counter and waved it like a conductor with a baton. "What does your husband call you?"

Becky flushed. "That's not the point."

"It most certainly is."

"Yeah, Becky, what *does* he call you?" Patty leaned on the counter, her chin in her hands.

"It's none of your business," Becky said primly. "Stella *offered* to tell us what Al calls her."

"Let's have it," Stella said cheerfully. "Or we'll get the drawings out of your room and hold your frogs hostage."

Becky's eyes grew big. "It's Cuddles, if you must know. And leave my frogs alone."

" 'Cuddles' and 'Sweet-ums'! I think I'm going to be sick," Patty groaned. "It's so sugary I feel cavities forming in my mouth as we speak."

"You three aren't helping," Jane said. "And quit eating the dinner before it gets to the table. Why don't you go into the living room and sit down and relax? We've all had a big day baking."

Jane shooed them out of the kitchen to carry on

214

their silliness where they weren't underfoot, and the sisters worked in contented silence until a rap on the back door startled them.

Lloyd Tynan, mayor of Acorn Hill and Ethel's special friend, pushed open the door.

"Lloyd, come in." Jane gestured him inside. "We're just getting dinner ready. Would you like to join us?"

"Thanks, but I can't stay," he said quickly. He nodded at the others. "Alice, Louise, good to see you. Mind if I sit down?"

Then, without waiting for an answer, he took a chair at the table.

Alice and Louise exchanged a surprised look. Lloyd seemed upset.

"I've come to ask you ladies some questions. I may need help." He drew a deep breath as if to calm his nervousness. "I'll cut right to the chase. Have you seen a change in Ethel lately?"

"She and Florence are making every effort to be neighborly to the new postmistress," Louise said.

"And they are outdoing each other in the good deeds department," Alice added.

"They were both working on layettes to give away when I stopped in to see her," Jane said.

Lloyd's brow furrowed.

"There are worse things than an abundance of good deeds," Louise pointed out.

"Ethel enjoys LeAnn. She says she has interesting opinions on things." He scowled a little.

"But she stops at my office with more speculation and gossip than ever before. Frankly, she seems anxious and upset."

"About what?"

"Mr. and Mrs. Billings, for example. She's sure that they've fallen behind on their taxes or some such nonsense. She told me that she knows that the IRS is hounding them. When I asked her how she had gotten that idea, she clammed up. You know Ethel. She can clam up pretty tight when she wants to."

The sisters nodded.

"Between this one-upmanship with Florence and her concern over people around town, she's just not been my Ethel lately."

"Perhaps I'll go to see her tonight," Louise suggested.

"Good luck." Jane smiled. "I tried to hint that they stop spreading rumors, and the two of them laughed and went right on with their business."

"I shall have to be more direct," Louise said calmly. "In fact, I'll do it right now." She stood.

"You'll miss dinner if you leave now," Jane said, glancing at the kitchen timer.

"I'll be back as quickly as I can, and I'll make do with leftovers if I must," Louise said gently.

Lloyd's face relaxed. "That sounds like a fine idea to me. Thank you, ladies. You've put my mind at ease."

Louise followed him out the door and walked

across the lawn to her aunt's home. She knocked on the door and waited, unlike her aunt who always simply opened the door of Grace Chapel Inn and walked inside.

It took Ethel some moments to come to the door. She'd been lying down. Her hair was mussed, and she was wearing her slippers instead of her shoes.

"If you are resting, I can come back later."

"No, dear, come in. I got up so early this morning that I felt a little tired. But right now, I'd enjoy your company." Ethel beckoned her inside.

As they had done so many times before, Ethel and Louise went directly toward the kitchen. Ethel filled the kettle and put it on the stove to heat, took out her tea things and filled a plate with Girl Scout cookies.

"You have Girl Scout cookies?" Louise sounded a little envious. Other than Jane's cooking, Girl Scout cookies were her only vice in the diet department. She would have dinner soon, but a few cookies couldn't hurt.

"I buy several boxes when I can get them. At my age, I've decided that once in a while it's acceptable not to have fresh baked goods in the house."

"That's fine at any age," Louise said. "If we didn't have Jane at the inn, Alice and I would eat very differently."

"She turned out well, didn't she?" Ethel said of

Jane. "Sometimes I ached for that girl, not having a mother to raise her, but we must have done something right."

Ethel, Alice and Louise had all cared for Jane when she was a child. It was a wonder, Louise thought, that Jane had actually stayed sane with all of them bossing her around.

"Such a cute little thing, she was," Ethel reminisced fondly. "Always off making something—a wreath of fallen leaves, a twig house or an elaborate drawing in colored chalk on someone's sidewalk. I believe the entire town of Acorn Hill watched out for her."

Louise cleared her throat. "That's why I've stopped by. I'm watching out for you."

"Whatever do you mean, dear? I don't need watching. Lloyd makes sure that things are going well for me. He's always fixing a leaky faucet or moving my lawn sprinklers, you know that."

It was true, but that wasn't exactly what Louise had meant.

"You haven't been at the inn much lately."

"You're full to overflowing over there. You don't need me underfoot too."

"But you have been busy, haven't you?" Louise suggested. "We still haven't gotten to know your new friend from the post office. You've been keeping her to yourself."

"Florence and I have kept her busy," Ethel admitted. "Florence finds her fascinating. She's much more . . . open . . . about her job than Alma Streeter ever was."

Louise stayed silent, waiting for Ethel to continue.

"I guess I have been a little distracted lately," Ethel admitted.

"Well, I want to catch you up on a few things. As you know, the rumor about Jean Humbert's going to Australia is false," Louise said. "And I wanted to warn you against mentioning Wilhelm Wood's trip to South America to anyone. Wilhelm's mother would be very upset if she heard that from someone other than Wilhelm, and he hasn't told her yet. She worries about him when he travels. It would be a shame if she worked herself into a dither over it."

Ethel looked concerned.

"You know, some of the news going around town could be hurtful if it got back to the people concerned. For example, the Billingses are doing just fine financially, thanks to their son-in-law who is an accountant with the IRS. They'd be very distressed if they learned that people thought they were in trouble with the government."

Ethel looked down at her lap and nodded.

Louise made a few attempts at small talk, but they were greeted with monosyllabic responses, and their conversation soon ground to a halt. Finally, Louise gave her aunt a kiss. "Take care, Aunt Ethel. Displaying fruits of the Spirit doesn't mean you have to provide for the entire world, you know."

Ethel smiled weakly.

Chapter Eighteen

The house had quieted down for the evening, and Louise slipped out to the front porch to enjoy the cool night air. The moon was out, and she could hear night creatures in the bushes orchestrating a sweet song. It was in moments like this that she couldn't imagine living anywhere except Acorn Hill.

A rustling off to the right captured her attention. The sound of shrubs being brushed aside and soft footsteps made Louise sit upright. Who was coming across the yard this late at night?

Louise's question was answered when Ethel's face, pale in the moonlight, appeared. She mounted the porch steps. Ethel was dressed for bed. She wore fluffy slippers and a robe that was pulled shut at the neck and belted tightly at the waist.

Louise lifted a hand in greeting but didn't speak. Being the oldest of the sisters, she and her aunt had always had a particularly close relationship. Her heart softened as she watched aunt shuffle up the steps and across the porch until she came to a rocking chair. She sat down heavily.

"Lovely evening," Ethel said finally.

"Indeed it is."

"Moon's out."

"So beautiful," Louise agreed.

They sat side by side in silence until Ethel began to rock.

Louise sensed that it was important that she not say anything yet. She began to rock as well. Eventually their swaying aligned itself. Back. Forth. Back. Forth. Louise wondered what her aunt had come to say, but was willing to give her the time she needed to get it out.

Back. Forth. Back. Forth.

Finally Ethel spoke. "Psalm thirty-four, verses twelve through fourteen."

Louise searched her memory for the verse. She'd learned a good many of them over the years. "Whoever of you loves life and desires to see many good days, keep your tongue from evil and your lips from speaking lies. Turn from evil and do good; seek peace and pursue it."

Although her senses perked up, Louise willed herself to remain relaxed.

Eventually Ethel's rocking slowed and she stood up. Without speaking she shuffled toward her niece and laid a kiss on the top of her head.

"Good night, dear."

"Good night, Aunt Ethel. Sleep well."

"I will." She disappeared down the steps, across the lawn and back to her own home.

She had just heard an apology of sorts, Louise knew, and she was sure that it had been difficult for her aunt to offer it. She smiled to herself. She had not directly told Ethel what harm her misguided gossip was doing, and Ethel had only indirectly confessed her wrongdoing. But it was as clear as if it had been written on a blackboard. Louise knew that now the odd bits of gossip would stop, and she would be very surprised if speculation reared its ugly head again for some time.

Lord, thank You for the sweetest, most endearing, most irritating aunt in the universe. We love her so much, and she loves us. Thank You for allowing us to have her in our lives. And Lord, will you please make sure she checks her facts before she starts telling stories in the future? Amen.

Then Louise rose and went to bed.

Chapter Nineteen

"My head is swimming," Jane announced to no one in particular. The three sisters were gathered on the front porch on Saturday morning. Stella and Patty had walked to town. Becky was upstairs calling home. Mary, exhausted from all the attention she'd received from townspeople, was sleeping.

"I'm wracking my brain to think of anything we've missed."

"We're keeping this simple, remember?" Alice said. "We've contacted the Potterston papers. We've baked a ridiculous amount of food. If we've forgotten something, we'll just make do. Besides, we've got Mary and Finn, and they're the most important part."

"You are right, of course. I suppose the only thing left to decide is who will present Kieran with his gift and explain Mary's situation. I won't be able to do it because I'll be busy with the food, going back and forth between the garden and the kitchen."

"And Alice and I will be pouring tea and serving the cold drinks," Louise pointed out.

"Then we really do need someone who can fill in the gaps and keep things moving," Jane said.

"Maybe Carlene could do it," Louise suggested. "She's talked extensively with Mary and understands the situation fully."

"But she'll be taking pictures," Jane reminded her.

"There's Fred Humbert, I suppose, but Vera told me that he'd be coming to the party late," Louise said.

"How about Wilhelm Wood? He's charming and well-spoken," Alice suggested.

"That's a great idea. I'll take a walk and ask him right now."

On the way out of the house Jane paused to look over the yard. It was as pretty as she'd ever seen it. God's gift of nature was so miraculous that she felt a tightening in her chest every time she considered it. Many times she paused to look at a new bloom on a hibiscus plant or watch a hummingbird dip deep into a flower for nectar and marvel at the intricacy of every living thing. Each plant and creature was designed to perfection for the job it was meant to do.

She picked up her step. This party would be fun. Friends, neighbors, flowers and tea. There wasn't anything much better than that.

Time for Tea was open, and Wilhelm was behind the counter sorting his mail.

"Good, you're here."

"Where else would I be?" He chuckled "I can't wait for your party. I'm looking forward to examining the butterfly garden you started. I might do one for my mother."

"She'd love it. I'd never realized just how many plants there are that butterflies enjoy. We've seen so many in our yard since I put in that garden."

He picked up a stool on his side of the counter and carried it to the other so that Jane could sit down. "Rest a little."

"I'm not even tired. This get-together has been fairly simple. My friends have been awesome. We're still baking, of course, but that's pure enjoyment for me. I love the excuse to do it. Between them and my sisters, it's been easy to pull this together."

"Everyone loves a mystery or a good pet story," Wilhelm observed. "This has both. How can anyone resist?"

"I hope that's true for you as well," Jane ventured.

Wilhelm cocked one eyebrow in her direction. "What does that mean?"

"Louise, Alice and I will be busy keeping things running on Sunday. At three o'clock we plan to ask Kieran to tell us how Finn behaved when he found Mary. Then Mary will say a few words. She's eager for people to know how it feels to wake up not knowing who you are or anything about your surroundings. We want people in the community to recall whether or not they saw anything that night that could help the police determine what happened. If we can jog just one memory, it would be wonderful."

"Sounds like you've planned it perfectly."

"The one thing I don't have is someone to introduce Finn, Kieran and Mary."

"You will be doing that, won't you?" Wilhelm pushed a stack of letters to the side and put his hands, palms down, on the counter.

"I could, but my sisters and I will be busy with hostess duties. Would *you* do it for us? I can't think of anyone better. You are charming, eloquent, articulate—"

Wilhelm burst out laughing and held up his hands as if to stop Jane's onslaught of compliments. "Enough! You had me convinced at 'charming.'"

He paused a moment in thought. "Should I tell a joke or two?" he asked, "if I promise not to tell any old, tired ones?"

"Whatever you think is appropriate," Jane said.

"Thanks, Wilhelm, this will free us up to give a great party."

She stood up to leave when he cleared his throat.

"I had an odd visit today."

"Oh?"

"Your Aunt Ethel stopped by this morning. We had a lovely but confusing conversation."

"What do you mean?" Jane asked cautiously.

"She appeared rather distraught. She told me she hadn't slept much last night, and that she knew she'd feel better once she'd talked to me."

"What did she say?"

"Frankly, I'm not quite sure." Wilhelm looked puzzled. "She carried on about misunderstandings and jumping to conclusions. She chattered about how very fond she was of my mother and that she'd never do anything to hurt her. She kept asking me if Mother was feeling okay. The next thing I knew she was vowing up and down that she would never, ever, make assumptions about anything ever again. She was quite distressed but eventually ran out of steam and just stood here looking up at me like a whipped puppy."

Poor Aunt Ethel!

"Then what?"

"I had no idea what she was talking about. I think she was apologizing for believing the rumor about my traveling to South America. Fortunately Mother never heard it through the grapevine, so I was able to break the news to her myself. No harm was done. After I told Ethel that, she seemed to relax. Next thing I knew, she was backing out of the door, smiling and waving." Wilhelm shook his head. "Odd. Your aunt is a sweet little thing. I've always liked her."

Thank You, God, for keeping an eye on Aunt Ethel and protecting her from herself.

On the way back to the inn, Jane was stopped by Nia Komonos, Acorn Hill's librarian. "Our library has been busy, thanks to you."

"What did I do?"

Nia laughed. "You've made everyone in town interested in dog stories, for one thing. And in books on amnesia. Everybody I've talked to is going to the party. Thanks to you, more than twenty books have been borrowed from the library."

"I guess that means that we can expect at least twenty people at the party. We'll find Mary's family yet."

Nia's dark eyes clouded. "How that poor woman must be suffering."

Mary felt safe at the inn with Alice and the rest, Jane knew, and the poor woman tried to put up a good front. But if she were forced to go out on her own right now . . . Jane hated to think of it. Mary was still so vulnerable.

As Jane continued down the street, Patsy Ley called out to her, "See you tomorrow."

Jane waved and smiled. Then she saw Lloyd

Tynan coming toward her. Jane knew a meeting with him would likely turn into a lengthy conversation. Hoping to avoid that, she slipped into Craig Tracy's flower shop. It was cool and quiet inside. Jane drew a deep breath and walked toward the counter.

"How do you like it?" Craig was arranging a colorful bouquet with roses, tulips, lilies and other flowers.

"It's marvelous. Is the lucky recipient anyone I know?"

"A couple in Potterston have a wedding anniversary today. Their daughter ordered this to surprise them."

"How thoughtful."

"Yes . . ." Craig kept working on the bouquet, but continued to chat.

"By the way, I met Jean Humbert in the Coffee Shop this morning and she told me a quirky story. She said your aunt stopped by the house and kept apologizing for this rumor going around about Jean having a boyfriend in Australia. Jean told her that she and her mother had had a good laugh over it. Jean's had a pen pal in Sydney since she was in sixth grade."

"Oh my." Jane's heart went out to her aunt, running around town, apologizing for something that even the people who were involved in didn't quite understand. *Not that I understand it all myself*, Jane thought.

"May I make a corsage for Mary to wear on Sunday?" Craig asked as he put the finishing touches on the anniversary bouquet. "Something to lift her spirits?"

"She'd love that, Craig. That's very thoughtful of you."

"Good. It will be my gift to her," Craig said. "I want her to know that I'm cheering for her. It must be very difficult to be in her position."

"Everyone has been very kind. I'm hoping that someone at the party saw something—anything—to help her learn her identity."

"People have certainly been discussing the situation."

"Gossiping, you mean?" Jane sighed.

"The joys of living in a small town. Really, people are curious just because they care."

Becky was coming down the stairs as Jane entered. Her face was flushed.

Becky flung her arms around Jane and gave her a boa constrictor squeeze.

"Whoa," Jane tried to wriggle out of her friend's embrace. "I'm having a little trouble breathing."

Becky reluctantly let go but took Jane's hand, led her into the sunroom, and gestured for her to sit.

"I just got off the phone with my publisher. Not only do they love the frog sketches I faxed to them, but they are willing to consider a children's book based on my paintings of Fairy Pond."

"Fabulous!"

"And I want you to promise you'll provide all the information I'll need once I start the book."

"Me?"

"Who knows Fairy Pond better than you? Louise said you know every species of every creature that lives there." Becky leaned forward intently. "Would you consider it? It would help me so much. This is my chance to both write and illustrate a book."

"I'm happy to try, Becky," Jane said. "As long as you aren't disappointed if I'm not as informed about Fairy Pond as you seem to think I am. Trust me, I'm no expert."

"But you love it and spend a lot of time there."

"Of course."

"Then start thinking positively, Jane. I know you'll be able to help me. No negativity is allowed."

Jane laughed. "You came to this reunion with some negativity of your own. Did something happen to change that?"

Becky sat back in her chair. "Several things, actually."

"Do you care to share them?"

"I came here so stirred up about Blaine that I could barely stand it. Should I kick my own son out of my house? How could I discover what's troubling him? What was I to do? I kept rolling it over and over in my mind, never finding an answer.

That was the problem. I've been trying to find my answer by relying on myself."

Jane tipped her head to one side and studied her friend.

"When I got here, I saw that you and your sisters put your trust in God every day. It's part of your way of living. He's not a God just for emergencies. You include him in all your decisions. It made me realize that I'd been praying on an as-needed basis, that I really hadn't entrusted Blaine to Him. I paid lip service to God but did I really trust Him to work this out? No."

Becky paused, but Jane sat quietly waiting for her to continue.

". . . so I decided to try it your way. At bedtime I've been reading Scripture—Psalms and Proverbs mostly—and praying. It is clear to me now that God is the only One to get through to Blaine, and He doesn't need my help to do it."

Becky flushed. "So I decided to turn it over. I prayed, 'God, Blaine's Yours anyway, so I'll get out of the way and let *You* take care of him.'"

Jane leaned forward. "And what happened?"

"I really did turn over my son, Jane. I know that I'll do whatever I'm led to do for him, but I'm not going to obsess over it anymore. I have heavenly help in my corner now."

Jane reached out to take her friend's hand. Sunlight spilled across their clasped fingers.

"I called my husband and we talked rationally

about Blaine. I told him what had changed in me. He promised he'd pray for Blaine."

"Amazing. When God is involved, remarkable things happen." No matter how many times Jane had experienced God's hand in her life, she was always filled with wonder.

"That's not the half of it. Blaine called me on my cell phone about forty-five minutes ago."

"*He* called *you*?"

"He told me that last night he'd had an overwhelming urge to talk to me. He wasn't sure why, but it was so strong that he finally decided he'd just dial my number."

"What did he say?"

"That he loved me." Becky's expression grew solemn.

"You don't look all that happy about it."

"My expectations were so high for my children." She looked pensively at a blue jay on the window ledge outside the sunporch. "Too high, apparently."

She was silent for a long while before she spoke again. "Blaine admitted that he froze when he tried to decide what to do with his life. He didn't want to disappoint us, so he kept going to school. It cost more and more money and he felt that he'd reached a place where it was too late to turn around and go back."

"What does that mean?"

"He went to school because he thought it was what I wanted, Jane. He wasn't doing it for himself, but for *me*." Becky's lips trembled. "Blaine has always loved animals and the outdoors. He said he always thought that the best job in the world must be to work on a ranch in the Southwest. He said he'd like to learn to train horses."

"Now, that is a switch."

"He's shut down because he can no longer follow a path I set for him, one he didn't lay out for himself."

"He's an adult. You didn't exactly force him to go to school."

"No, but can you imagine what I might have said if he'd announced he was dropping out of college to go to New Mexico and learn to rope and ride?"

"What would you have said?"

"I would have cried and stormed around the house and told him he was throwing his life away."

"And then?"

"Eventually I suppose I would have gotten used to the idea, realized that Blaine knew his own heart and encouraged him to go." Becky gave a teary smile. "And I probably would have decided that I should do some paintings in that part of the world, do a children's book in the Southwest, be wildly successful, buy my own ranch . . ."

Jane held up her hand as she laughed. "You don't have to wind it out quite that far. But you would have accepted his decision and let him go?"

"Of course."

"Then Blaine got it wrong too. He decided what

you'd think. Didn't he? He chose the path he thought you'd like without regard to his own wishes."

"I meddled too much in his life. He was always a child who wanted to please me. If I hadn't been so controlling, none of this would have happened."

"He loved you enough to want to honor your wishes. That's admirable, Becky. It's your communication that fell apart. You made very big assumptions about each other."

"We did, didn't we? We're going to talk when I get home. There's so much to sort out. I told Blaine that if he needed to pursue his dream, that he should do so. The school won't go anywhere. He can always come back to it. He needs to know more about himself to make that decision."

Becky smiled tremulously. "Do you know what he said to me, Jane? He said, 'Mom, we should have had this conversation a long time ago.'"

"Sometimes God waits until we clear a path through our attempts to solve things. When we finally turn things over to Him, He can do the healing and blessing that He's been waiting for and wanting to do all along."

"And when I finally asked Him to help Blaine—and me—He was there, ready, willing and waiting," Becky marveled. "You know, Jane, if I travel for the rest of my life, no trip will ever stack up to this weekend."

Chapter Twenty

Mary knocked timidly on the partially open door to Jane's room. "Is this a good time?"

Jane waved her in. "It's always a good time for you. Go to my closet and pick out whatever you want to wear. If you can't find something here, Alice offered her closet too."

"I've never known such generosity . . ." Mary paused and smiled. "I don't think."

"Has anything else come back?"

"Things are beginning to seem . . . familiar. I hear songs that I recognize from somewhere in the past. It feels as though my memory—my personality— is hovering just below the surface, waiting to emerge."

"Then it will. We will just have to be patient."

"I'm just about out of patience," Mary said. "And there's not a thing I can do about it."

"Perhaps if you can manage to relax and enjoy the day, something will come to you unexpect- edly."

"I guess it's worth a try."

Jane opened her closet door. It was, as Alice had said, as if a rainbow had exploded inside.

"How will I ever choose?" Mary gasped. She touched the soft fabric of a black silk dress, then reached for the next garment, a long flowy skirt.

"Choose what?" Stella and Patty had come

upstairs to chat with Jane. Stella wandered into the room blowing little puffs of air on her fingernails to help them dry.

"What she'll wear to the garden party tomorrow."

"Does this mean we're going to have a fashion show?" Patty asked.

"Sure. Get Becky. We might as well do this by committee."

When her four fashion judges were seated, Mary went into the bathroom, slipped on a pale blue dress, came out and turned gracefully for the others.

"Pretty but not bright enough," Stella said nodding. "You'll be competing with a lot of flowers, you know. We want you to show up in the crowd."

"I don't think I'm a very showy person," Mary said shyly. "At least I don't *feel* showy."

"Let's see another one," Patty ordered, getting into the spirit of things.

Mary disappeared and came out in a little black dress.

Becky whistled.

"You look fabulous in that but it's too dark," Stella pronounced. "Let's see another."

"I think we need chocolate to make this decision," Patty announced. "Something to fortify us." She walked out of the room, and they could hear her footsteps descending the stairs. By the time Mary changed and came out again, Patty had returned with a plate of Jane's homemade truffles in her hand.

The party mood escalated from there. When Mary appeared in a colorful tie-dyed skirt and a military looking jacket with epaulets, they were all laughing.

"I'd better step in, or we're never going to find an outfit," Jane announced. "I may have just the thing." Instead of going into the closet, she knelt on the floor and pulled a dress box from beneath her bed.

Jane put the box on the bed and removed the lid. A cloud of tissue paper billowed up. She reached in and lifted out a sapphire blue sheath with Asian styling. She held it up and let the smooth silk fall to its full length, then held it up to Mary. The color brought out her eyes. "This is one of my favorite dresses," Jane said, smiling. "I wore it to a number of gallery openings, and it never failed to get a compliment."

"I couldn't borrow this. It's too beautiful!" Mary reached out and touched the smooth silk.

"That's why you *should* borrow it."

Mary looked longingly at the dress.

"You can't say no," Jane instructed. She turned to the fashion gang lounging on her bed. "Ladies?"

"It's you, Mary."

Mary looked hesitantly at Jane who nodded.

A puzzled expression flitted across Mary's features. "I think I just remembered something."

She suddenly had four rapt listeners.

"It's this color . . . I had a dress this color once, I'm sure I did." She closed her eyes. "I was small, I think. It feels like I was small but . . ." Her eyes flew open. "I lost it again."

"It's a good sign, Mary," Becky assured her. "It means the memories are coming back."

A smile lit Mary's face. She looked at Jane. "I would be honored to wear this dress. Thank you."

"We're going to do an intervention," Becky announced as Patty and Jane sat in the sunroom playing a game of checkers.

"Let me guess," Patty sighed. "What's Stella doing now?"

"Another facial. Or a scrub. Or some sort of exfoliation. The woman spends more time on her skin than I do on my career."

Becky leaned over Patty's shoulder and made a move with one of Patty's checkers. "Have you noticed? She never comes out of her room unless her makeup is done and her hair is perfect."

"Are you talking about me?"

They all turned to look at Stella as she walked into the room looking as if she'd stepped from the pages of *Vogue*.

Becky blushed, but Stella smiled and joined them in the room.

"You don't understand," she said, taking a seat on a wicker chair. "You can all do your business in private. Becky, you have a home studio. Patty, people expect you to be in working clothes when you are at their homes. Jane, people would think it odd if you wore high heels every day. It's not that way with me. My studio is upstairs above our gallery."

She looked straight at Patty. "That's what I envied most about you, Patty, all of you really. None of you ever worried about how you looked."

"Yes, we did," Patty said, touching her hair unconsciously. "You just worried more."

"You did seem to spend a lot of time in front of the mirror," Becky said quietly.

"My mother always said that we are judged on first impressions." Stella sighed. "The underlying message was that if I wanted to be liked, I'd better look good."

Jane reached out and touched Stella's arm.

"My father ran a tight ship at our house," Stella said quickly. "When he came home from work he wanted the house tidy, dinner on the stove and my mother wearing a dress and earrings."

Stella looked down at the floor. "Dad had very fixed ideas about how things should be. Women should be thin and beautiful. Children should be seen and not heard. And any daughter of his had better represent him properly. Any time that I stumbled or made a bad decision, Dad took it personally."

"We never knew," Becky murmured.

"I never liked him very much back then. I *loved*

him, but I didn't like him. I didn't agree with his strict rules. He had rules about everything—how I dressed, how I wore my hair, even my friends." She looked down at her hands. "He was very judgmental, but he was also my *father*."

Stella remained silent for a long moment. "I know we're supposed to honor our parents, but it's not always easy. Frankly, I looked forward to leaving home and going to school. I longed to be free."

"I'm so sorry, Stella," Patty breathed.

"But you're still listening to your father's voice in your head," Jane said.

Stella turned toward her.

"You're still living by his rules, aren't you?" Jane looked into Stella's eyes, and Stella quickly looked away. "You think there's a certain way you have to look, to act, to be," Jane said. "You're trying to make someone happy who isn't here any longer."

"I don't think . . . maybe . . . but . . ." Stella looked truly puzzled. "Am I?"

"What does your husband say when he sees you in the morning?" Patty asked.

"Al says I'm beautiful. He thinks I'm perfect the way I am."

Jane laughed. "So let me get this straight. You are trying to live up to an image that you've had in your head since you were young. You feel you'll never be good enough, yet you live with an *art connoisseur* who sees beautiful things and people every day and who says you're perfect." She smiled at Stella.

"Why don't you listen to *him* for a change?" Becky asked.

"Your husband sounds like a smart man to me," Patty said.

Stella appeared genuinely bemused, as if what she'd always believed to be reality was really smoke and mirrors.

"How did your parents feel about growing old?" Becky asked curiously.

"*Hmm?*" Stella said vaguely. "They hated it. Especially my mother. She knew how much Daddy cared about how she looked. It's odd, though. After he passed away, she started wearing blue jeans and funky shirts and threw out all her high heels. Once I caught her emptying her bathroom cabinet of makeup. She said she'd decided to go natural."

"How did she look?"

"She looked her age. She didn't try to hide her crow's-feet. She was really . . . beautiful. Graceful. Happy." Stella looked at the faces of her friends. "I guess Daddy's stern ways affected her too."

"I think that makes sense," Jane said quietly.

"Now she lives on the beach and walks in the surf every day. She's active in community functions. And she refuses to dress up for anything except church on Sunday."

They were all so silent that they could hear a

clock ticking somewhere in the house and a wood-pecker hammering on a tree outside.

"We loved him, you know. In so many ways he was a wonderful father and husband. He was generous, hardworking, reliable. I always felt safe with him. I knew that he would never let anything happen to me. He taught me to ride a bike and to change a tire. If I had run into trouble at school, he would have driven across the country to help me out." She looked out the window.

Suddenly Stella stood up. "I've got to think. I'm so confused . . ." Before anyone could stop her, she walked out of the room.

Patty, Becky and Jane stared at one another. Finally Patty spoke. "Boy, have I had things wrong about Stella."

Wendell, who had been sleeping soundly on a pillow on the floor, woke up, yawned so deeply everyone could see right down his pink throat and leapt into Patty's lap.

"Hey, big guy," Patty murmured as she scratched behind his ear. Wendell meowed once, turned around twice on Patty's lap and lay down.

"Looks like you have a new friend," Becky commented as the cat promptly closed his eyes and went back to sleep.

"Good," Patty brushed her hand slowly across Wendell's soft fur. "I need every one I can get."

Chapter Twenty-One

Early on Sunday morning Jane stretched in the sunbeam that played across her bed. Wendell, who had sneaked into her room when she'd retired the previous night, was also stretching lazily at the end of her bed. He extended himself to his full length and even spread his toes as he roused himself from a good night's sleep.

"Ah, kitty," Jane murmured as she reached to scratch his exposed belly. "If only we could all be as relaxed and content as you." He rumbled a purr in reply.

Today was the garden party. Jane pushed her fingers through her hair and placed her bare feet on the floor. There was a gentle tapping on the door. Alice walked in and handed a cup of coffee to Jane.

"What time is it?"

"Early. I couldn't rest any longer. I believe I was counting lemon bars in my sleep."

"It's not that big a party," Jane said. She picked up a robe from behind the door, put it on and then sat down on the bed to enjoy the coffee. "But it's so important to Mary. Perhaps we've raised her hopes too much that someone will come forward with a clue to what happened to her."

Alice frowned. "Mary has so much hope that someone will have seen something."

"We've done all we can." Jane sipped the

steaming coffee. A smile pulled at the corners of her lips. "At least we're not worried about having a good crowd. You know how people are here. They love a party."

"And goodies," Alice reminded her. "Maybe that's why I couldn't quit counting those lemon bars. I hope there are enough."

"We have plenty." Jane put down her cup and reached for the hairbrush on her bedside stand. "I think it will be fun, don't you? Patty, Becky and Stella are looking forward to it. They are eager to meet more of the locals. In their minds, Acorn Hill is a picture-perfect town." She stroked the brush through her hair. "That notion isn't far off, actually. We do live in a lovely spot."

"It's been quite a week, hasn't it?" Alice asked. "It seems impossible that we've accomplished all we have—quilting, baking, visits to Fairy Pond, caring for Mary. You have some amazing friends, Jane. I feel like I know you better, having heard their stories about you. I hope they will come back again."

"I hope so too. It's been a wonderful time for me. And for the others too, I hope." Jane gave a wide yawn and another catlike stretch that would have made Wendell proud. "I suppose I'd better get moving. I want to walk through the gardens to make sure no weeds raised their unwelcome little heads overnight."

"By the way, Pastor Ley and Patsy offered to

come early and do what they could. I gave him the assignment of making sure cars didn't park every which way. We don't need a traffic jam."

"Good idea."

"Pastor Ley said he'd direct some of the people to park in the church parking lot."

"Perfect. This is working out rather well, isn't it? We may have to make it an annual tea party."

Another knock on the door announced Louise's arrival at the early morning get-together. She, too, was carrying a cup of coffee for Jane.

"My my, how do I rate?" Jane accepted the second cup, since she'd almost finished the first.

"You've been so dear and generous about Mary that it seems only appropriate that you deserve a little pampering yourself. That's why I took it upon myself to find some music for our tea party."

"I never even thought of that. I suppose if we were to have a real garden party we'd need some strings or a harp."

"Fortunately we can do something much simpler than that. I found some wonderful harp music on CDs. We can set a CD player beneath the serving table where it is hidden by a tablecloth. It will provide a little atmosphere."

"That sounds lovely, Louise. By the way, I talked to Craig Tracy for a moment yesterday," Alice added. "He is bringing Mary's corsage this afternoon after he delivers flowers to the hospital in Potterston."

"Maybe I don't have to get out of bed after all," Jane said. "Sounds like you've taken care of everything." Jane stared pensively out the window at the morning sky. "When things unfold so easily I can sense God's presence, can't you?"

After breakfast, Jane found Patty on the front porch holding a mug of coffee and staring off at some distant point. She leaned against the porch rail to study her friend.

Patty finally noticed Jane watching her. "How long have you been there?" Patty's hair was soft and golden in the sunlight, framing her face like a flaxen cloud.

"Just a few moments. You were certainly lost in thought."

"I've been lost there a lot this week."

"Still thinking about Stella?"

"I feel like such a fool. What I assumed was cockiness and overconfidence in her was insecurity. Because of my jealousy I ruined a relationship between her and someone she loved."

"When are you going to talk to her?"

"I don't know." She sighed. "It's been so busy that none of us have had a moment alone. I've waited this long. I can certainly wait until later. I want this afternoon to be perfect for Mary."

They both turned when they heard Sylvia Songer coming up the steps. She wore white linen slacks and a coral silk shirt.

"Hi, there. I just met Viola. She said that the Coffee Shop was buzzing with excitement yesterday. Everyone was trying to think of something they may have seen on the day of the accident. I think your problem might be too many sightings, not too few." She laughed. "I hope people don't begin to imagine they saw something."

Sylvia peered into Patty's nearly empty cup. "Is there more where that came from?"

Jane disappeared into the house and returned with a mug, a carafe of coffee and a plate of powdered doughnuts.

"Oh, this hits the spot," Sylvia said as she nibbled daintily on a doughnut. "I ran into Wilhelm Wood on his way to his store."

"At this hour? On a Sunday?"

"He said he needed to gather a few notes for this afternoon. I think he's pleased to help out." Sylvia took a sip of coffee. "I do hope we'll find out something about Mary. I know it's going to be a lovely party anyway, but if no one comes forward it will be disappointing."

"As Alice said this morning," Jane said softly, "the situation is in God's hands. We'll have to trust Him."

Ethel came out of her house with a watering can to water the moss roses encircling her mailbox. She looked surprised to see the gathering on the inn's front porch.

Jane waved her over. "What are you wearing to the party, Aunt Ethel?"

"I don't know yet, dear. I'm thinking of my yellow dress. Lloyd likes it." Ethel blushed like a schoolgirl. "Is Mary up?" Ethel asked. "I have something I want to give her today. I crocheted a bookmark for her with a little white cross. I purchased a Bible for her and made the bookmark to put in it."

"How nice of you, Auntie."

"Not so much nice as necessary, really. We need to care for those less fortunate than ourselves. Don't you agree? Sometimes I care a little too much," she said cryptically, "but my intentions are always good."

With that, she moved off again, faster this time, and disappeared into her house.

"What was that about?" Sylvia asked. "The part about her intentions being good?"

"You never quite know with Aunt Ethel, do you?" Jane answered. "Shall we go inside and see if the others are planning to go to church?"

After church and a light lunch, the women of Grace Chapel Inn fluttered about, getting ready for the party.

"How do you like this?" Stella came out of her bedroom after lunch and pirouetted in the hallway. She was wearing a hot pink dress and brightly colored jewelry. "Is it festive enough?"

"You look like a party all by yourself," Jane said.

"My husband likes me in pink." Stella studied herself in a hall mirror. "I look okay, don't I?"

"More than okay."

Stella followed Jane up to her bedroom. "After our conversation yesterday, I feel like a load has been lifted from my shoulders."

"I hope that you never forget you are beautiful, inside and out."

Stella turned to Jane with a look of deep gratitude. Jane smiled, then held up two dresses.

"Which should I wear, the navy or the orange?"

"Orange. You always did like bright colors. Be yourself." With that, Stella flitted out of the room and downstairs to check on Becky.

Grace Chapel Inn became part dressing room and part fashion show as everyone prepared for the party. Louise put on a full beige linen skirt, a dressy pale blue silk blouse and her signature pearls. Alice changed clothes three times before settling on a white piqué skirt and a peach blouse.

Mary was the only one who didn't take part in the chatter in the halls or gather with the rest of them in the living room. She stayed in her room with the door closed.

Sylvia, who had promised to come early and help set the tables, arrived a little after one o'clock.

"Don't you ladies look wonderful?" Sylvia said. "Like a bouquet of brightly colored flowers." She looked around. "Where is Mary?"

A noise on the staircase got their attention, and they all turned in that direction.

Mary stood shyly at the center of the staircase, her hand on the railing. Jane's bright blue dress skimmed her slender figure perfectly. Her hair, which she'd worn pulled back most of the time she'd been at Grace Chapel Inn, was down, softly framing her face.

Becky gasped, Patty clapped and Stella pronounced her "fabulous." Alice hurried to the stairs and took her hand. "You're beautiful, Mary."

"I feel like a little girl playing dress up." She drew a shaky breath. "I hope this works."

"Don't worry if our little party doesn't turn up something. Let's hope that the piece in the *Acorn Nutshell* or one of the larger papers will turn up some leads. Word will spread," Jane said.

"Today is as much about wanting you to know we're with you as it is about anything else. You do understand that, don't you?" Alice said quietly.

"I'm sorry." Mary smiled wanly. "Sometimes, when I think about it too much, I feel paralyzed with fear. Right now I should be telling you how grateful I am for all you've done, but there aren't words enough to express my thanks."

Alice leaned close to Mary. "Our reward will come when we find your family."

Chapter Twenty-Two

I'll start the music," Louise announced and bent to flip the switch on the CD player beneath the serving table. The sound of a harp floated into the yard.

Alice gave the flowers a last look, and Jane began to brew pots of tea and turned on the coffee urn. Wendell posed in the window, unmoving and so regal that he cut an impressive figure.

"How does it look?" Jane asked when the beverages were ready and she had returned to the yard. She was glad she'd done a lot of fertilizing earlier in the season, because now the flowers were thick and vibrant.

"It's lovely," Louise said.

Stella came out of the inn followed by Becky and Patty. Shortly afterward, Sylvia Songer rounded the side of the house and joined them in the center of the yard.

"I saw Lloyd knocking on your aunt's door," Sylvia said. "And there are several people walking down the street toward the inn. They kept looking at their watches to check the time. I suppose they don't want to be early but refuse to be a minute late either."

"Surely Acorn Hill knows the concept of an 'open house.'" Stella's brow creased. "Everyone doesn't have to come at the start and stay until the bitter end."

"I wouldn't count on that," Jane said with a laugh.

Sylvia peeked beneath a thin white dishtowel spread across a basket to see what goody was beneath. "*Mmm.* Pecan tassies." She put the towel back in place. "Florence was parading down the street with her husband and the postmistress LeAnn in tow."

"Where's Mary? She should be down here to meet the guests." Alice bustled off to round up their guest of honor.

"Where are Finn and Kieran? I'd hoped they'd come early so we could visit before everyone else arrived." Jane glanced toward the street.

Patty had gone to the front of the house to see who was coming down the sidewalk. She returned to answer Jane. "They just pulled up. You'll never believe how cute they both are. Did you realize that Finn's fur and Kieran's red hair are just about the same color? They both look as though they've been showered, shampooed and conditioned within an inch of their lives."

Finn and Kieran did look wonderful when they appeared in the garden. Kieran wore a bright green shirt and Finn had a matching scarf around his neck. The big dog had a happy expression as his tongue lolled out one side of his mouth.

Wilhelm Wood caught Jane by the sleeve and gave a little tug.

Jane turned. "Oh good, you're here. And don't you look handsome?"

"Will I do?" Wilhelm was dressed in a pair of navy trousers and a shirt so white Jane thought she might need her sunglasses to look at him.

"Perfect. I'm so glad you agreed to help us out. My sisters and I will be kept busy with the food and drink. Oh look, Kieran and Finn are already socializing."

Kieran looked proud enough to burst his buttons as an audience gathered around him while he retold the story of trying to call Finn home and of the dog refusing to budge from his spot near Mary.

"I don't know how long it might have been before anyone found her if it weren't for my dog," Kieran said. "I always knew he was a smart dog but I had no idea . . ."

Jane and Wilhelm smiled at each other. Things were off to a rip-roaring start.

"There's nothing for you to do until we start our little program," Jane began, "so just mingle and enjoy yourselves." She glanced at the table and her eyes widened. "The plates are already emptying. I'd better get busy."

A sudden hush fell over the gathering group. Jane looked up to see what had happened, and saw that Alice was ushering Mary over to where Finn stood with his owner. Finn held his head and ears high, taking it all in. When Finn saw Mary, he broke away from Kieran and headed directly for her.

They met in the middle of the yard and to everyone's delight, Mary embraced the big dog. Finn responded by licking Mary's cheeks.

A few people clapped, and there was a ripple of laughter.

Rev. Thompson tapped a spoon on the side of a pitcher of iced tea. "If we can all bow our heads for a moment, I think this is an excellent time for a prayer.

"Dear Father in heaven, thank You for the bright sunshine, glorious flowers and sweet fellowship today offers. We ask that someone, somehow, will help Mary discover her identity—if not today, in Your own perfect timing. Bless the people of Acorn Hill, our families and precious friends. Amen."

"Amen," echoed those standing about.

The afternoon sun warmed the yard as people drifted around and enjoyed the refreshments while chatting happily with their neighbors.

Clarissa Cottrell was there, keeping an eye on her cake, cutting additional slices when needed. Vera and Jean Humbert talked animatedly with Craig Tracy, and Pastor Ley and his wife Patsy moved easily through the gathering. Mary was chatting with a reporter from Potterston, who was scribbling frantically in a notebook.

LeAnn had managed to free herself from Florence's orbit to stroll through the yard with Hope Collins.

"This is a wonderful idea, Jane," Hope said,

moving toward her. She gestured in the direction of the new postmistress. "You know LeAnn, don't you?"

"Yes, we've met in the post office. How are you enjoying Acorn Hill?"

"It's a pleasant little town." She smiled, her brown eyes crinkling up at the corners. "Friendly." She pronounced. "Extremely friendly."

She glanced over at Florence, who was carrying a plate on which was a healthy selection of dessert bars and cookies. Her husband Ronald, his balding head shining in the sun, trailed a few steps behind her. They drifted across the yard to find chairs in the shade.

Jane looked at Florence and back to LeAnn. "Florence and my Aunt Ethel are a little overenthusiastic, but they mean well."

"Your aunt is a sweetie," LeAnn said. "I guess I'm just not really used to small-town life yet."

Jane tipped her head to indicate she was listening.

"I had no idea that people were so interested in one another."

"What do you mean?"

Hope chuckled. "LeAnn's not used to the gossip in a small town. She's not accustomed to everyone knowing one another and actually being interested in what's going on," she said, taking a bite of her lemon bar.

"Fortunately I've learned my lesson," LeAnn

said and made a zipping motion across her lips as she glanced in Florence's direction. "If you know what I mean. And Alma will be back in a few weeks, so I guess it's just as well.

Before Jane could respond, Finn discovered Wendell sitting in the window and began to bark, causing a commotion. Jane started for the house to fix the situation, but was waylaid again.

"What a wonderful party you've organized," Florence said, appearing out of nowhere. "I see you were talking to LeAnn."

Jane nodded.

"When LeAnn came to Acorn Hill she was very lonely, you know." Florence frowned. "A little *too* lonely, perhaps."

"What do you mean?"

Florence glanced around and then leaned forward so only Jane could hear. "She was so desperate to meet people and make friends that I think she *talked* a little too much. She said things. Not much, mind you, but enough to get you thinking. She hinted, for example, at who was getting interesting mail from faraway places and if a lot of unusual mail was going to one address, little things like that." Florence looked disapproving. "She shouldn't do that. It's how rumors can get started, you know."

Florence looked as innocent as a newborn babe. "People in this town are trusting. When someone tells us something, we think it's the truth, not speculation or half-baked supposition."

Jane bit her tongue. She was not about to point out to Florence that she and Aunt Ethel had been just as eager to receive and dispense information as LeAnn had been to give it.

"Anyway, it looks like LeAnn has found a friend closer to her own age," Florence said, nodding toward LeAnn and Hope chatting by the tea table. "I think we did a good job of being neighborly, don't you?" With that, Florence dismissed the gossip fiasco. She waved at her husband, who was still seated in the shade. "Come on, Ronald. Don't dally. I need more tea."

Jane shook her head and started for the house again, but Louise came up behind her. "Look who stopped by," Louise said.

Jane turned to see their former houseguest Claire and her husband Ben standing nearby. Claire looked relaxed and happy.

Jane went up to Claire. "I'm so glad to see you here."

"We were driving through town, saw a sign at the gas station and had to stop. We couldn't miss it, not after knowing Mary personally," she said, taking her husband's hand. "I still can't believe that I was actually at your place when Mary came. Has anyone had a clue to her identity yet?"

"Not yet, but we have hope." Jane smiled at the young couple.

"I thanked Louise for all that you sisters did for me—and for Ben," Claire said to Jane. "I behaved horribly, but he forgave me." She turned shining eyes on him. "That's what really told me how much he loves me."

Ben gave a lopsided grin. "I think we've both come a long way toward growing up."

Jane left the couple smiling at each other, and then slowly made her way to the other side of the yard. Mary was standing there with Finn. She and the dog looked as if they'd been best friends forever. Finn looked up at her with liquid brown eyes, and she smiled down at him and gently stroked the top of his head.

Wilhelm stood beside them, glancing at his wristwatch. "It's three, Jane. Do you want me to start?" He ran his finger beneath the collar of his shirt.

"Nervous?"

"Not really." He smiled. "These people are family to me, to all of us. Just a twinge of stage fright to keep me sharp."

"Excuse me, excuse me please!" he spoke loudly into the crowd. Gradually conversation quieted, and soon he had everyone's attention.

"Our hostesses have asked me to say a few words. As you know, Mary was discovered about a week ago not far from Fairy Pond. Her memory has not yet returned, and Louise, Alice and Jane have invited you today to share in the hospitality of the inn, and to ask that if you—or anyone you know—saw anything, *anything* that might be even remotely connected with Mary's situation, that you come forward. You might have seen an unfamiliar car, a stranger, someone parked by the side of a road . . ."

Jane looked across the yard as she listened. The guests were paying close attention to Wilhelm. Lloyd and Ethel were leaning forward and listening with such intensity that they looked like they were walking into a strong wind. Carlene Moss was taking notes for her article and Pastor Ley had his eyes closed—praying, no doubt.

Jane's heart swelled with affection for these wonderful people who cared so much for a complete stranger.

By the time she returned her attention to Wilhelm, Mary had joined him. She had Finn's leash in her right hand and Kieran's hand in her left. When she spoke, her voice was soft but clear.

"This is the most wonderful opportunity for me to say thank-you to my rescuers," she began. "You all know my story by now, but perhaps you don't know that I was unconscious when I was found. I don't know how long I might have lain there or what might have happened to me had not Finn and Kieran come along. I believe I owe a huge debt of gratitude to Finn for finding me and sensing that I was in trouble, and to Kieran for respecting and paying attention to his dog's instincts. They are both heroes in my book."

Clapping erupted as well as a few cheers and whistles.

Kieran blushed the color of his hair.

Mary held out the gift that Jane had purchased. "This is a token of appreciation to you, Kieran. My gratitude is heart-felt." She turned to glance at Alice. "And we have something for Finn too."

At Mary's signal, Alice pulled a net bag of doggie accoutrements—bones, dried pigs' ears, toys, a box of flavored treats and even a plaid hat with holes where Finn's ears would go—from behind the tea table.

Finn's tail began to wag as Alice opened the bag and tossed him a rawhide bone. Completely, blissfully unaware of the attention focused on him, Finn lay down in the grass and began to chew.

"The Howard sisters are my other heroes. They took me in and generously shared their home without any expectation of compensation." Mary smiled ruefully. "Unfortunately I don't have a dime to my name . . . and I don't, for that matter, have a name . . . but I give them my eternal gratitude for the love they've shown me."

The guests again began to applaud.

Then Wilhelm stepped forward to wrap up the formal part of the party. "Be sure to greet Mary, Kieran and Finn, folks, and if you can think of anything that might help us, we'd all be so grateful."

Jane was about to return to her hostess duties when Aunt Ethel suddenly appeared beside her.

"Hello dear, what a lovely party." Her hair shone brightly in the sun.

"Are you and Lloyd having fun?"

"Oh my, yes. He's so proud of the people of Acorn Hill and how they've supported Mary."

Ethel put her hand on Jane's arm. "I just wanted to tell you, well, you know . . . it was all a misunderstanding, of course. It was unfortunate but we . . . wanted to make friends, you know . . . it seemed right at the time. I'm glad you said something . . . I just wanted you to know." Then Ethel brightened. "Did you know that Florence and I are going to be knitting baby afghans for the church? It's our new project." She smiled. "Oh, Lloyd is waving at me." She gave him a quick wave, then turned back to Jane. "I have to go. It was nice talking to you, dear." Ethel moved off, leaving Jane to ponder the mysterious conversation. Jane's heart filled with affection. Her dear, sweet, funny aunt. Life in Acorn Hill would be boring without her.

The sun hung low in the sky when the last stragglers finally left the party. Stella, Becky, Patty and the Howard sisters set to work quickly, and soon the lawn and kitchen were back in order.

"Let's sit down and enjoy the garden before we put away these last chairs," Jane said, looking around. "I think we deserve a few minutes with our feet up."

The fragrance of the flowers, the scent of freshly cut grass, and birdsong surrounded them.

"Did anyone come forward with new information about Mary?" Becky asked quietly.

"No." Mary shook her head. "Not yet."

Louise's eyes flew open, and she looked at Mary's crestfallen face. "They still could, you know. Someone will tell someone about the party who will tell someone else, who will . . ."

"It was a wonderful party," Mary said with feeling. "You have all tried so hard to help me."

She squared her thin shoulders. "But I do think it's time I faced the fact that I might not recall or find out who I am for a long time. I guess I have to get on with my life."

"What will you do?" Patty asked.

"I've been thinking about it," Mary said. "I'll need to find a place to live, and I'd like to stay in Acorn Hill. People have been kind to me here. If I can find a job, and then a place to live, at least I will have friends." She looked shyly at Alice, Louise and Jane. "Like you."

"I think that's a splendid idea," Louise said. "Don't you agree, Jane?"

"Absolutely. But I wouldn't give up hope that your memory will come back. With time . . ."

"I know, but until then, I want to be in Acorn Hill." She put the tips of her fingers together and rested them beneath her chin. "I think I landed here for a reason. Even in my darkest moments, God has had His hand on me." Tears came to her eyes. "But that doesn't mean I'll quit praying for my family to come and get me—if I have one."

"Maybe we should go inside," Jane suggested as the light began to fade. "I've got a casserole to put in the oven. We all need something to counteract the truckload of sweets we've consumed today."

"Great idea," Becky said, and stood up. "I'm on a sugar high. I don't even remember how many brownies I ate. I was cutting them in the kitchen and the row was always crooked so I'd have to straighten it. You wouldn't want crooked brownies, would you?"

"I felt the same way about the lemon bars," Patty admitted. "I had so many that my teeth started to squeak."

"Teeth can't squeak."

"Yup, they can. Mine did."

One by one they meandered into the house.

"I'll set the dining room table," Alice volunteered. "The rest of you can go upstairs and get into something more comfortable."

"I wish we didn't have to leave tomorrow," Stella said. "This has been one of the most wonderful vacations of my life—wonderful friends, a beautiful location, fine dining, mystery and intrigue . . ."

"And don't forget the quilts," Becky said.

". . . and creativity and learning."

"It has been nice, but I'm almost looking forward to going back home," Becky said wistfully. "In fact, I think I'll give Blaine a call before dinner. I want to see how he's doing." She glanced at Jane. "No meddling, I promise."

Before any of them could climb the stairs to the second floor, however, the doorbell rang. Two uniformed policemen stood on the porch.

"What is it?" Jane asked when she saw their somber faces. "Has something happened?"

Chapter Twenty-Three

We're looking for the woman with amnesia." The officers stepped through the door that Jane held open for them.

"That's me," Mary said nervously.

"Officer Briggs, Ma'am. And this is Officer Perry. We're with the Potterston police. We've discovered something relevant to your case." The policeman reached into his pocket and pulled out a driver's license and handed it to Mary. "Does this look familiar to you?"

Mary stared at the small rectangle. "The picture looks like me. It says this is someone named Lorna Carver . . ." She drew a sharp breath. "Is that me? Where did you get this?"

"We think we've figured out something. Is there somewhere we can speak in private?"

Mary looked around at the faces of the women she'd come to care about. "These women deserve to hear what happened too," Mary said quickly. The officers nodded.

"You'd better come in and we'll all sit down," Louise suggested. She led them into the living room. Everyone sat, creating a strange, anxious tableau as they waited for the officers to continue.

"An accident report came in late this afternoon," the shorter, huskier officer named Briggs said. "Someone reported a car on its side at the bottom of a ravine about five miles north of Acorn Hill."

"When we got to the site, we saw that it was not a recent accident," said the taller, fairer officer. "The car had been in the ravine quite a few days. It's a heavily wooded area, and the vehicle landed in a location that isn't easily seen from the road. If it hadn't been for the hiker who ran across it, it might not have been discovered for many weeks."

"Is that my car?" Mary whispered.

Officer Briggs nodded and continued. "We believe that after the accident you walked to the point where you collapsed. You must have gone nearly four miles from where the vehicle went into the gully. We aren't sure how long you were by the side of the road, but it's fortunate that the dog and his owner came along."

Mary stared at the driver's license in her hands. "So this is who I am?"

"We believe so." The policeman cleared his throat. "We did find some other items in the car. A suitcase, maps and a journal. From what we can gather, you were on a trip to Florida."

Mary continued to stare at the driver's license, tears in her eyes.

"We contacted the people at the address on your driver's license. They had assumed that you were traveling at first. Then when you didn't show up, they reported you missing. That was three days after you left home."

Mary looked up and clasped her hands to her ribcage. "Oh my." Then she took a deep, steeling breath. "It's what I've wanted. Why do I suddenly feel so afraid?" Mary—*Lorna*—sounded as if she was having trouble getting out the words.

"It's quite natural to be afraid of the unknown," Jane said gently.

"Now what?" Mary asked.

Officer Briggs continued his story. "It seems you hadn't been on the road long. Your home is only about eighty miles west of here. Your family started out as soon as we contacted them. They're waiting outside."

The silence in the room was absolute. Finally Alice broke it by saying, "What are we waiting for? Let's bring them inside." Then, realizing that this was Lorna's decision, she turned to her and added, "If you're ready, that is."

"I don't know when I'll be more ready," Lorna said uncertainly.

The two officers rose and went to the door.

". . . or more scared."

Officer Briggs returned to the house, leading a

man and a woman and two teenage boys. The tall gentleman was in his early fifties. There were furrows in his brow, but his eyes shone with kindness. The woman, Jane realized, looked a good deal like Lorna. So did the two jeans-and-T-shirt clad boys, who were obviously twins.

"Lorna!" The man took a step forward and then stopped himself. "They said I shouldn't go too fast. I don't want to frighten you, but we've been so worried."

"This is Jerry Carver, Ma'am, your husband." The police officer looked ill at ease. Obviously it wasn't often that he had to introduce a wife to her husband.

"Husband?" Lorna stared at Jerry. "But . . ." She looked down at her bare left hand.

"You'd lost a lot of weight recently," Jerry said softly, holding out a gold ring. "It was too loose. You were going to have it resized."

Lorna took the ring from his outstretched hand and examined it. She smiled at him weakly. She closed her hand around it and waited.

"And I'm your sister Mazie," the woman stepped closer. "And these are your boys, Kent and William."

Lorna stared at the youngsters, gangly teens shuffling from side to side, obviously wondering what to do with their hands—and their emotions. A smile brightened her features. "I have sons?"

"We don't want to rush you." Mazie looked to the

officer for direction, then back to her sister. "This must be terrible for you. We love you, Lorna, and we're so sorry this happened to you. Just tell us what you want us to do."

The boys squirmed under their mother's intense examination until one of them exclaimed. "Quit staring, Ma! You're making me nervous."

Everyone burst out laughing, breaking the tension in the room.

"French Fry," Lorna blurted unexpectedly.

Jane and the others exchanged concerned glances, but Lorna's family didn't look surprised.

"French Fry and Big Mac!" she said delightedly.

The boys grinned from ear to ear.

"Frenchy and Mac!"

"What does it mean?" Alice asked gently.

"I don't recall my sons yet, but I remember our cats!" She was half laughing, half crying. "It will come back," Lorna said, now assuring her family. "Frenchy and Mac are Siamese kittens. If I know that, the rest is bound to follow." She moved forward and held out her hands to her husband and sons. "Now that I've found you, I can wait patiently for the rest."

Jane smiled and backed out of the room, gesturing for the others to follow so that Lorna could have time with her family.

Chapter Twenty-Four

It was after ten when Lorna's family left the inn, assuring her that they would be back in the morning.

"Are you certain you don't want to go along?" Alice inquired. "They seemed very eager to have you go with them."

"Even though I *know* they are my family, I don't remember them," Lorna sighed. "I've got to ease into it." She looked around. "Right now *this* is the only home I remember. Thank you, Alice, for offering to drive me to Potterston in the morning. It will be good for my family to meet with the doctor. It will help them understand what's happened to me."

"How about you, Lorna? Are you okay?" asked Alice. "Really okay, I mean. A lot has happened for you today."

"I'm fine. Much better than I was before I knew that I had a family." She hesitated briefly. "They seem nice, don't they?"

"They're wonderful. It's obvious how much they love you and how frightened they were while you were missing."

"I don't understand why they didn't report you missing immediately," Becky said.

"Apparently I'd been on my way to visit my sister in Florida." Lorna shrugged. "I was planning to take my time driving. My husband . . ." she smiled a little at the word on her lips, "was out of town on business, and the boys were staying with friends. Jerry had been leaving messages on my cell phone, but no one was at home to check in with me, and Mazie didn't expect me right away. Each thought the other was in touch with me. I guess I just fell through the cracks for a few days." She shuddered. "I really fell through them, didn't I?"

They all smiled.

"Once my husband and the boys returned home and realized none of them had heard from me, they called my sister. She hadn't heard from me either. By that time, I was already here at the inn. They realized I was missing and panicked."

"Are you going to put on your wedding ring?" Louise asked quietly.

Lorna pulled it out of her pocket, where it had been since her husband gave it to her. "It doesn't fit." She slid it on her finger to demonstrate. "Apparently one of the reasons I was so excited to see my sister was to show her how much weight I'd lost."

"At least now we know how you got all the scratches and scrapes," Alice said. "You'd been making your way through trees and brush trying to get out of that ravine."

"If I'd been on the road, I might have been seen earlier, the police said, but because I followed the bottom of the gully, no one noticed until I made it to the road where Finn found me."

"You have no idea how worried we were that you'd been dropped off there on purpose and . . ." Jane's voice trailed off.

"I couldn't think of a reason that anyone would leave me there unless they wanted to get rid of me." Lorna shook off the thought. "But everything has turned out all right." She smiled. "I don't really remember my husband, but I already *like* him. My family will be here for me while my memory returns."

"You're on your way. Remember French Fry and Big Mac."

Her gaze traveled over the women and rested for long moments on each of the sisters. "God bless you people. You did a wonderful thing for me." Lorna put a hand to her lips. Too choked up to speak, she turned and went upstairs.

"I'm so exhausted that I'm not even taking off my makeup before I go to bed." Stella drooped dramatically against the banister.

"What about your pores? Aren't you afraid of having them plug up overnight?" Becky teased.

"Tonight I'm going to live dangerously."

"What a risk taker," Becky muttered, "living on the edge."

"What a weekend," Stella sighed. "I can't imagine that anything more exciting than this could happen."

• • •

Monday morning Jane had coffee brewing by five. After mixing a batch of scones to bake and putting out jars of orange marmalade and raspberry preserves, she glanced at the clock. It was early, and she'd given everyone strict instructions not to set their alarms, so she didn't expect to see anyone downstairs before nine. She knew her sisters were sleeping soundly because she'd checked on them before she'd come downstairs.

That was why Jane was surprised to see Stella tiptoeing into the kitchen carrying her running shoes.

"You're up early."

"I'm wired from last night. I thought a nice long run might burn off some of my excess energy. Want to come?" Stella sat down on a stool and slipped on her shoes.

"Are you kidding? I'm not going to do anything more strenuous today than walk upstairs to take a nap." Jane pushed a cup of fresh coffee in Stella's direction.

"It's been an amazing week, hasn't it?" Stella savored the aroma of the brew before taking a sip.

"Remarkable."

"It's changed things for me, you know. Until this weekend I had no idea how completely I was still listening to my father's voice in my head. He was a good man, Jane. Misguided, yes, but I believe he tried his best."

"You forgive him?"

"I'm starting to wish I'd done that much earlier in my life." Stella rolled her eyes. "It would have made things a lot simpler."

She clapped the palms of her hands against her thighs. "I'd better get going, or I'll convince myself not to do it. I'll be back in half an hour or so."

"Have fun," Jane said to Stella's receding back.

Jane poured herself another cup of coffee and broke open a cranberry muffin left over from the day before. She'd eat again when the others awoke, but she expected that to be a couple of hours later.

She watched the birds flock around the feeders as she waited for the oven timer to ring. Then she took the scones out and laid them on the counter. She was surprised to hear more footsteps on the stairs. This time Patty entered the kitchen. Her blonde hair was uncombed, and she still wore her pajamas. There were dark rings beneath her eyes. She looked worn out.

"Did you sleep?"

"If I did, I can't recall it. I tossed and turned like a fish on the bank."

"Too much excitement?" Jane handed her a scone and a cup of coffee.

"Last night was wonderful. All the turmoil was in my head after I went to bed."

"Stella?"

"I have to tell her, Jane. Time's running out.

We're leaving this afternoon." Patty groaned. "I have to get it out, but I'm dreading it so much."

"She's out for a run. Why don't you catch her when she comes in? That way the two of you can talk in private."

"I want you to be with us."

"Wouldn't it be better to do this without me?"

"She won't strangle me if you're watching."

Jane chuckled. "So I'm supposed to protect you? Frankly, I don't think you're in much danger, my dear."

"I'd still feel better if you were with us."

"If you insist. But I think you should do it alone."

"Do what alone?" Stella asked from the doorway. She was panting and there was perspiration on her forehead.

"You weren't gone long," Jane said.

"I didn't go very far," Stella said sheepishly. "I've really let myself slip this week. I felt like I was running through mud. Do you have any more coffee?"

"Gallons." Jane filled a cup.

"Now what is it Jane wants you to do alone?" Stella said to Patty as she joined them at the table. She reached for a scone, broke it open and spread it with butter. When she looked up her eyes were sparkling. "Real butter. No more margarine for me. I'm going to live a little."

"I have something to tell you," Patty began, "and Jane knows what it is. I asked her to stay with us because . . . you might want to scream at me, and I know that we all behave better when we're around Jane."

Jane rolled her eyes. When had she become the manners police?

"I can't think of a thing that would make me want to do that," Stella said frankly. "This week has made me realize that I love you guys more than ever."

"Maybe you'll want to take that back when I'm done," Patty warned.

Stella stared at her, comprehending the gravity of Patty's mood. "What is it?"

"Remember when you were going with Barry when we were in college?"

"Yes." Now Stella looked really confused.

"You loved him, didn't you?"

"Well, yes, but what does that have . . ."

"You might have married him if the two of you hadn't had that terrible fight, right?"

"We'd talked about it," Stella admitted. "Of course, we were awfully young."

"Have you kept track of Barry over the years?"

Stella smiled. "Actually I have. It took a long time, but we were finally able to talk again. He's done quite well for himself. He owns a manufacturing business. They make gadgets for airplane engines, I think. He's a pilot himself. He owns a of couple airplanes. He's still good-looking too, better, actually, than he was when we were in school."

Patty groaned. "It's worse than I thought then."

"What on earth are you talking about?" Stella nibbled on her scone.

"Barry is handsome, successful . . ."

". . . charming, debonair, and the father of five children. Can you imagine? Five!"

"I was hoping you'd say he was chubby, bald and delivered newspapers for a living."

"You have got to tell me what this is about," Stella ordered. "You're upset, and I have no clue why."

"Remember the day you and Barry broke up?"

Stella rolled her eyes. "How could I forget? I haven't been in a bigger argument before or since. He was furious with me and I with him."

"Over the lost necklace?"

"I didn't lose it," Stella said firmly. "Something hap-pened to it, but it wasn't my fault. Of course Barry didn't believe that. He acted like I'd tossed it in the trash."

A flicker of sadness passed over Stella's features. "Frankly, that's why I reconnected with him. I needed him to know that wherever that piece of jewelry went, it wasn't my fault."

"It *wasn't* your fault," Patty echoed.

"I know but . . ." Stella looked at her oddly. "Why are we having this conversation?"

Patty dipped into the pocket of her pajamas and pulled out the necklace. She laid it on the counter between them. "It was *my* fault, Stella. I'm the reason you and Barry broke up."

"Don't be ridiculous. And where on earth did you find that necklace?"

"I've had it all along—since we were in school."

Stella registered this information in slow motion. "If that's the case, why didn't you give it to me back then? You could have saved me a million tears."

Patty drooped like a thirsty flower. "I didn't give it back because I was the one who took it."

"Took it? You mean you . . . intentionally . . . why?"

"Because I was so jealous of you and Barry. I thought I loved him, but he never even looked at me. He only had eyes for you. Stella, I'm ashamed to admit this, but I was so jealous of you back then that I could *taste* it. I took it because I knew that it would cause trouble between you and Barry. But when it caused you to break up, well, I knew I'd gone too far, but it was too late to admit what I'd done."

Stella looked at Patty as if she were speaking a foreign language.

"You had it all: looks, brains, personality and Barry. I wanted to hurt you."

Tears streamed down Patty's cheeks. "I am so sorry for what I did. I was all wrong about you. You were hiding so much pain, and all I saw was your shell, not your heart. And now you'll never speak to me again, and this friendship we've renewed is ruined."

The situation was so uncomfortable that Jane wanted to turn away from Patty's pain, but instead, she put a hand on her friend's shoulder.

"Who says it's ruined?" Stella asked.

Patty's head snapped up. "What?"

"Who says it's ruined?"

"How can you even look at me after what I did to you?"

"What, exactly, do you think you did to me?" Stella was remarkably calm.

"I ruined your life, that's what. If I'd stayed out of it, you and Barry would probably have married. You'd be the one with five children and a huge house and . . ."

"Five children? I don't think so. And a huge house? Patty, have you ever seen my home? Al and I are going to sell it because it's too large for us. Stuff doesn't matter to me. Love is what matters."

"And I messed it up for you because I was eaten up by jealousy."

"Patty!" Stella said firmly, "look at me!"

Patty lifted her head.

"You have been blaming yourself all these years for ruining my life? Patty, you probably did me the biggest favor in the world."

Patty narrowed her eyes. "I don't understand."

"If I'd married Barry, I never would have found and married Al." Stella leaned forward. "All that business with Barry is history, water under the bridge. Sure, I was devastated for a while, but not nearly long enough."

Now both Patty and Jane looked at Stella questioningly.

"If I'd been as deeply in love with Barry as I thought I was, I wouldn't have been dating someone else within six weeks. My wounds would have taken considerably longer to heal, don't you think?"

"But I meddled in your life . . ."

"Yes, you did, but without that meddling, I may never have met Al. He's been my anchor throughout my career. Barry didn't care about my work. He always joked that he didn't understand it. Do you think I would have been happy married to a man who didn't respect my art? Al, on the other hand, admires me both professionally and personally. He's crazy about me, Patty, and I feel the same way about him. Barry wasn't the one for me. I would have discovered it sooner or later. I understand that now. You just made me figure it out sooner. If he broke up over something as absurd as my losing a necklace and refused to believe me when I said I hadn't misplaced it, why would I want him?"

"You aren't furious with me?"

"Oh, I'm disappointed, I guess." Stella put her hands on her hips. "It's not what you expect to hear from one of your closest friends. But it's the past, Patty." Her expression softened, "Besides, I can see that you've suffered enough. There's nothing I could do or say that's worse than what you've done to yourself. I see the pain in your eyes. I wouldn't have punished you for all these years."

Patty stared at Stella, slack-jawed. Then she tipped her head back and groaned. "You aren't going to yell at me? Tell me you'll never speak to me again?"

"I always knew it was you who was keeping the four of us from getting together," Stella said. "I never knew why, because you'd see Becky and Jane separately but . . ."

"I didn't want to see you because it brought up all the remorse I felt."

"Frankly, I'm glad to know why it happened, Patty. I never understood."

"You never said anything."

Stella gave a wry laugh. "Remember me? The girl who wanted to be perfect? I always thought you didn't want to see me because of something I did. Patty, I'm actually happy to know what happened. I thought I was to blame."

Patty looked at Jane, who was quietly slicing fruit into a bowl. "You've got something tumbling around in your head right now, don't you?"

"Funny, isn't it, how the Bible speaks to everything, to every situation?" Jane said mildly.

"Let's hear it," Patty sighed.

"Proverbs 10:9: 'The man of integrity walks

securely, but he who takes crooked paths will be found out.' "

Patty looked from Jane to Stella and back again. "If it weren't for me, we could have had weeks like this every year. I'm so sorry."

"Then we'll have to start making up for it," Jane said. She put her hand on Patty's arm. "That means *you* plan our next reunion."

"When's the next one?" Becky shuffled into the kitchen in her slippers and pajamas. "Tell me right away so I get it on the calendar. Let's make it at a time I'm not under deadline . . ." She paused, seeing the streaks of tears on Patty's face. "What's going on here?"

"It's a long story," Jane said, shaking her head. "But a good one."

Chapter Twenty-Five

Louise, Alice and Lorna found the others already at the dining room table when they came down for breakfast. They were looking at old photos Jane had dug out of a trunk.

"I suppose it's time to start bringing the suitcases down so we can load the van," Stella said with a sigh.

"I don't want to leave," Becky said glumly. "This has been too perfect." Then she brightened. "But Jane and I will get together soon. She's going to help me with a book I'm writing on Fairy Pond."

"Can we join you?" Stella asked. "You'll be much more creative with us around."

Lorna watched them without speaking.

"What's going on in your head, my dear?" Alice asked. "You're thinking so hard I can practically hear you."

Lorna put her arm around Alice's shoulder. "I was wondering about the people I call my friends. Could they possibly be as wonderful as all of you?"

"I don't see why not. Like attracts like, you know," Alice said.

"I'm still frightened," Lorna admitted. "I'm glad I now have an identity, but my life . . . I just don't know."

"From now on you'll have us too," Alice reminded her. "Perhaps you and your husband or sister can come back for a visit."

"I'd like that." Lorna's chin quivered.

Before she could say more, someone knocked at the front door.

Alice went to open it and was met with a gigantic bouquet of flowers that nearly filled the doorway. Craig Tracy's face peered through the greenery.

"Delivery for 'The Women of Grace Chapel Inn.' "

"For us. Why?"

"I guess you'll have to read the card to find out." Craig came through the open door, marched into the dining room and set the floral arrangement in the middle of the table.

Louise plucked a small, white envelope out of the mass of blooms, opened it and read aloud the enclosed card.

> *To the caring women who kept our*
> *Wife, mother and sister safe.*
> *We will always be grateful.*
> *Lorna's Family*

Lorna looked as delighted as if she'd been the one to receive the flowers. Her face glowed as she announced, "They *are* as nice as I'd hoped they'd be. How thoughtful."

"And grateful," Alice added.

"Generous too," Jane commented, eyeing the size of the bouquet.

"Looks like you have a winner of a family," Stella commented. "And we know that they're fortunate to have you."

Lorna burst into happy tears, and, as if on cue, every one of the women began to dab at her own eyes. Craig carefully backed out of the dining room and onto the porch, then closed the door quietly behind him.

That evening, the three Howard sisters sat once again on their wide front porch and watched the daylight fade.

"It's going to be very quiet around here without all our guests," Louise said.

"I already miss them," Alice added. "It's a good thing we have reservations for next weekend.

"How do you feel, Jane? It's been an especially challenging week for you."

Jane looked out across the lawn and toward the little town they all loved. "I feel grateful. I wondered if I'd feel restless or dissatisfied when I saw my old friends and heard about what they were doing. Instead I feel peace. This *is* where I'm supposed to be, and it's where I'm happiest."

"It's where we all belong," Louise said with confidence. "It's where God has planted us."

Alice nodded emphatically. "All we have to do here is grow."

"Amen," her sisters said in unison. "Amen."

Paper Bag Apple Pie

SERVES SIX TO EIGHT

<u>Filling</u>:
1 unbaked nine-inch piecrust (homemade or
   ready-made)
6–7 cups (about six apples) tart apples, peeled,
   cored and cut into thick slices
½ cup granulated sugar
½ teaspoon cinnamon
2 tablespoons flour
2 tablespoons lemon juice

<u>Topping</u>:
½ cup brown sugar
½ cup flour
½ cup butter

Place unbaked crust in pie pans.

Prepare apples and put in bowl. In a separate bowl, combine sugar, cinnamon and flour. Gently combine flour mixture with apples, and spoon into piecrust. Sprinkle with lemon juice.

For the topping, combine brown sugar and flour, and then cut in the butter to create a coarse mixture (about the size of peas). Sprinkle mixture evenly over the top of the apples.

Slide pie into a brown paper bag (like a grocery

store bag), and fold the open end over twice and secure with large metal paper clips. Bake on a cookie sheet at 425 degrees for one hour. Carefully split open the bag and allow pie to cool on wire rack. (Cooking inside the paper bag helps the apples to heat thoroughly without overbaking the crust.)

Guideposts magazine and the *Daily Guideposts* devotional book are available in large print editions by contacting:

Guideposts, Attn: Customer Service
P.O. Box 5815
Harlan, Iowa 51593
(800)431-2344
www.guideposts.com

Center Point Publishing
600 Brooks Road • PO Box 1
Thorndike ME 04986-0001 USA

(207) 568-3717

US & Canada:
1 800 929-9108
www.centerpointlargeprint.com